THIRTEENTH MOON
A STAR'LITE FANTASY

j. SNODGRASS

Information and other Writings
misterjsnodgrass.wordpress.com
amazon.com/author/jsnodgrass

j. SNODGRASS

Design and Layout by Al Feville

ISBN: 9781094742564

THIRTEENTH MOON
A STAR*LITE FANTASY

J. SNODGRASS

For Elizabeth, who bought me a copy of The Golden Bough.

Humbly submitted to Sir James Frazer, Robert Graves, Riane Eisler, Joseph Campbell and, naturally, to Daniel Quinn.

Thank you Michael, Mom, Jack, Justin, Carly, Melissa, Peter, Anthony, Melinda, Marie, Lauren, Jamie, Tom, and Brett.

"I am a stag: of seven tines,
I am a flood: across a plain,
I am a wind: on a deep lake,
I am a tear: the Sun lets fall,
I am a hawk: above the cliff,
I am a thorn: beneath the nail,
I am a wonder: among flowers,
I am a wizard: who but I
Sets the cool head aflame with smoke?

I am a spear: that roars for blood,
I am a salmon: in a pool,
I am a lure: from paradise,
I am a hill: where poets walk,
I am a boar: ruthless and red,
I am a breaker: threatening doom,
I am a tide: that drags to death,
I am an infant: who but I
Peeps from the unhewn dolmen, arch?

I am the womb: of every holt,
I am the blaze: on every hill,
I am the queen: of every hive,
I am the shield: for every head,
I am the tomb: of every hope."

-Druid Chant
(Arranged by R. Graves)

"Beyond the rim of the star-light,
my love is wand'ring in star-flight
I know he'll find in star-clustered reaches...
strange love a star woman teaches."

-G. Roddenberry

Cave painting, France, c1300 BCE

THIRTEENTH MOON

"Peet?" the curlibird's chirp flicked through dawntime silence as the sun's first rays combed across the purple forest of Deia. "Peet? Peet?"

The melody would have been quite pleasant to human ears but the lyric, if translated from bird, was a bit distasteful, especially this early in the morning: "Spray it on your eggs I'm gonna." Even among curibirds this particular song was considered extremely vulgar - "Peet" is, after all, a four-letter-word.

Silence. Then the forest lazily rustled, awakened, and commenced its dawn pageant. Trees uncurled their variously purple fronds for the morning feed. Hungberry bushes retracted their leaves and clenched their bunches. Flowers slouched seductively and put their scented genitals on display.

"Peet?" the curlibird launched its lusty call again.

On the glistening limb of another tree, a gurlibird poked her sharp head out from the steaming-fresh carcass of a jackanape and responded: "*Re*peet."

Things were about to get nasty.

♭

Ra*shrump,* ra*shrump,* ra*shrump,* a shaggy blue creature limped through the wood on two massive hooves. It hobbled into a clearing, froze and glanced around in fear, its long beard swirled and antlers whistled in the wind.

Stillness, silence.

The creature peered deep into the forest, large owl eyes unblinking. It was being hunted.

Then, a thin whine from a black speck above. The whine grew to a hiss, crackling and sizzling, deepening and widening as the object ripped a trail of smoke across the sky. Closing in on the glade, the hiss deepened to a bellowing roar, the large object charging like a bull.

Ra*shrump*-ra*shrump*-ra*shrump*, the monster lurched off into the forest.

Tree-limbs shattered and leaves rustled unexpectedly into confetti flight as the pod smashed its way through the canopy. Then with a thunderous noise it burrowed, heaving half into the forest floor. With this thrust it threw pieces of itself all over: large clunkering hunks, medium clattering chunks and a zillion tiny tinkling plinks. Momentum spent, it settled and sizzled. Then it peed out some oil and lay pathetically dead.

A light drizzle of leaves.

Stillness, silence.

"Poot?" another curibird chirped. "Poot?"

Stillness, silence.

A gurlibird answered, "Noot." This conversation had not gone well.

♭

The escape pod hissed as a battered hatch half-opened and a female face peered out. Wide black eyes in Egyptian skin, brows and cheeks and lips like a sculpture smoothed by centuries of sandy breezes, a button-nose that looked sort of popped-on as an afterthought, all framed in bobbed tendrils of spiral-wirey black hair. Her eyebrow twitched.

Hinges groaned and whined as the hatch stubbornly resisted a push, then gave up altogether and thudded to the leafy ground.

The boxy grey button-down and black skirt of her Interstellar Syndicate uniform were badly tattered, but with a steely expression she took a soldier's step forward. And she toppled down.

Her eyebrow twitched.

One by one her limbs remembered themselves, a hand clawing the dank soil, a foot pushing against a bush, another hand pulling her forward into the glade. Tender purple grass and foamy blue moss, the sound of a brook nearby, she dragged herself four strong heaves toward it, and collapsed.

Stillness, silence.

"Peet?" the unsuccessful curibird finally ventured again.

Stillness, silence.

ß

An ensign nimbly hopped down from the pod and surveyed the surrounding woodland. He sniffed at the forest – lavender, the calming scent of lavender like they sprayed in academy bathrooms, but more lush and electric, more real.

Crouching in the brush, he darted his dark brown eyes around. His broad, bronze-colored face, when serious, was a mask of three slabs – a forehead and two cheeks that hung like heavy stones. But there in the midst of the sweet-smelling purple forest, he couldn't help but smile, and the stone slabs of his cheeks scrunched into dimpled, golden-brown marshmallows. The crash had disturbed his dense black hair, shiny locks curling in rebellion against the Syndicate slick.

He let out a calm breath and the forest relaxed back into its early-morning genetic commerce – the meat-market was open. Curibirds chirped and skrotes chattered, a frisky breeze invited the flowers to sway in a hypnotic dance. Even the tree-trunks had the faintest hint of seductive writhe about them.

Seeing the navigator unconscious in the moss, he cautiously stalked into the glade. But as he approached her, the forest gasped into silence. A scent on the breeze alerted him to swivel on his heels and stand at full attention. On his tippy-toes a bit.

It was the Captain.

ƀ

"Captain!" the ensign saluted.

Calvin Theseus Falco, handsomer than all the marble-carved statues of himself, radiating a personal musk that perfumers around the galaxy struggled in vain to synthesize. "At ease, ensign. Status report?"

The ensign quickly wiped the corner of his mouth – how embarrassing. "Our escape pod was knocked off course by a chunk of the ship, then battered around in the asteroid field. I don't know what planet this is, and the processors are beyond repair."

Sandy brown hair in perfect formation, hazel eyes that changed with his mood and a jawline that had been registered in the transgalactic trademark office. "An escape pod..?"

"You hit your head on the steering console when the Exogamy took her first impact."

The grey button-down and black kilt of his uniform were standard issue, but looked meticulously tailored to his sleek dancer frame. Falco stood precisely five foot eleven and a quarter, and his jackboots elevated him to a perfect six feet. "I don't feel...injured..."

"Your head is fine, the console was completely demolished. Without your lightning instincts the ship was drifting out of control and getting pulverized. It was protocol for an ensign to drag you onto a pod, she followed you."

"...My ship..." Falco looked slowly up and out, his two-thousand-lightyear stare penetrating the sky as his body gracefully shifted into eulogy-stance.

"Captain. Request permission to--"

"Exie..."

"*Why* were we speeding through an asteroid field? *All* of the charts said 'asteroid field' when we were *sixty thousand kilometers* away - and closing in. Now the ship is destroyed and--"

"...Gone. I was in the academy when she was built. Bony and scrappy with hundreds of workers handling her inner parts, I would gaze out the window during...pointless history lectures and say, 'No matter how many times these guys nail and drill you, nobody will ever know you the way I will.' As first officer on the shuttle Proboscis when she was christened, I took shore-leave and watched an admiral...pop a champagne bottle on her big, round, powerful rear-engines... I've never formally admitted this, official charges were dropped, but...that night I knocked out the personnel guarding the ship, went to the bridge and...told her how I felt. And urinated on the captain's chair. Then I broke into the admiral's house and urinated on *him*, just so there'd never be any mistake she was *mine*. She was planned to me, in the stars, in the reverberations of the first supernova. I've explored uncharted females all over the galaxy but there *is no love* like the love between a captain and his ship."

"Captain, this is very...informative...but *she* may need medical attention."

Falco cocked an eyebrow quizically, then realized "she" could also mean the unconscious navigator. "She's a fembot. If she doesn't reactivate in four minutes, give her a slap on the backside."

"...That works?"

"It works with my coffee-maker and I think they're manufactured on the same planet. My *ship* is...dead..."

"I was there."

"All we have left is..."

"Each other."

"The pod. Ensign, what's the status of the pod?"

"It won't fly. Communications are out, *we* were way out from Syndication space. How will they find us?"

"When I fail to file a captain's report the Syndicate will disperse my pension to sponsor a shareholders' gala. Fortunately I still owe Federation-Loan six billion spacebucks in academy debt. When I miss my next payment, they'll send a Collector to get me working again or...sell my pelvis to a museum."

"When is your next payment due?"

"Not for almost a year but don't worry. They once dispatched a collection officer to spring me from a maximum security asteroid."

"Where you'd fooled the Globulon warden to put you in deep confinement with the spunky Space-babes of Saturnalia! I read the story you wrote in Captain's Log magazine. But I didn't know how you'd escaped."

"I'd spent months...formulating a plan. It takes time when you're trapped in a cell with eighteen alien hookers, some of them can survive on human sweat. But before I could initiate my escape the cell door blew open. A collector, dripping a rainbow of blood, threw me in a bag over his shoulder and battled his way out. When the bag came off I was back in the captain's chair, transferring a late payment. With collection fee."

"My father wouldn't let me take academy loans. I had to work my way through, walking hybrid pets. Got hospitalized by an iguano-rangutan-garoo...ended up in debt anyway."

Falco's attention partially returned from the cell and the space-babes. "So it all worked out in the end."

"I know this may not be the best time, but..." The ensign pulled a tiny comic book from his shirt pocket, "could I have your autograph?"

"I always have time for a fan." Falco pulled out a holo-monacle to magnify the book, "Ah yes, the Big Dipper in Deep Space Double Issue." He inscribed it 'to my good friend' then paused and squinted at the ensign, "Hey, you're not selling these, are you?"

"No, *sir.*"

Falco jotted a letter F and handed it back, "Right – you say that every time I sign one."

"We've never met, sir."

"Oh?"

"Ensign Claudio Rivera, security, first month on the ship. My name came up for landing party on the Gargantua Nebula but the Crisco vaccine gave me an outbreak of pimples. The dispatcher said I wasn't up to handsome-standard for a mission."

"You're the lucky one then. All the handsome security officers I brought down were baked into a living pie and eaten by King Corpulus. I was only spared by order of his daughter Obessa. 'Obessa," Falco quoted from his story, "'she made me wish I had bigger eyes...'"

"'And bigger hands.'" Claudio joined him to complete the line, "Yes, in Starbuck magazine issue four sixty-two, 'That's No Moon.' I've read all your stories. My favorite is the 'Sponge Sisters of Seraglio-sphere.' Is it really true? The triple exfoliation?"

Falco's lip curled, "They can scrub the meat off a man's bones. Fortunately I'd...just been moisturized by the mud-maidens of Meteor Omega."

A female voice from the ground groaned, "Captain..."

"Captain, she's reactivating."

"Where *are*--" As Claudio approached she rolled over and arose, "Oh my stars, what happened to my uniform!?" Cascading tatters of a black skirt bashfully clung to her powerful thighs. Shreds of a grey button-down strained against her aerodynamic abdomen and courageous bust.

Averting his eyes too late, the ensign tried to blink out the image. "It must have ripped when a meteor tit the-- Hit the shipple. Shuttle."

"But you two were in the *same crash* and your clothes are fine."

The ensign's boxy grey shirt and pleated black skirt were fine, but permanently wrinkled from accomodating his build, shorter and broader than Syndicate standard. "It's true, I've never seen poly-sci-fiber tear like this – have you, Captain?"

"It doesn't." Falco coolly responded, "Crewette uniforms are pseudo-polyester, designed to shred on dangerous missions. Helps to bolster morale during a crisis. Ensign, this is Donna Trankh, our navigator--"

Ignoring the ensign, Donna leaned at the Captain, "What 'crisis' is helped by having a crew-member exposed, objectified?"

"What do *you* care about objectification? You're a fembot - you *are* an object."

She gasped, and her arms momentarily lost track of grasping for modesty. "I am *not* a fembot."

"...*What?*"

"I've told you *before* I'm not a fembot. Your *last* navigator was a fembot – *I'm* a woman."

Falco squinted incredulously. "...But you know so much about navigation..? And you're so pneumatic and compliant--"

"I know navigation because I studied it for six semesters. And I said yes after the Easter social because I thought... Wait - you thought I was a fembot. That whole night?"

"Of course. I never would have...*engaged*...if I thought you were a *biological* crew-member. I'm open minded but *that's* just *creepy*."

"But I *told* you I wasn't a fembot. I said 'I'm not a fembot, Captain.'"

"Yes, *all* fembots say that when you unwrap them – that and 'Is that how you like it, Captain?'"

Donna drew herself up, "I never said *that*."

"I assumed you were malfunctioning. And fembot malfunctions are... Well *dangerous* but not something you just turn away from."

Just then the ensign shouted "Captain, look out!" and sprung to protect him. Falco gracefuly side-stepped and Claudio fell into the moss.

Swiveling on his heel, Falco eyed the approaching monster. *"Finally. Something that makes sense."*

ß

Hobbling irregularly, the blue shaggy beast lunged into the clearing. It was the shape of a man, but with great hooves for hands and feet, and an enormous dangling wang. Big owl eyes flashed on Falco and Claudio, then fixed on Donna, and it lowered its head to charge at her with the seven points of its antlers.

She instinctively lunged, shielding Falco with her body, and try though he might, the Captain couldn't get past her. Claudio launched from the ground and drew his pistol but the monster knocked it from his hand, crushing it to pieces with a mighty clomp. Then it swung a hoof that sent the ensign spinning.

"Ex*cuse* me please," Falco said, attempting to brush Donna aside.

"Stay behind me, Captain!" she shuffled him back with her elbow before throwing a punch the creature narrowly dodged.

"It's *just* a *space-monster* – I'll *handle* it!" Falco barked sternly. He'd beaten quite a lot of these.

Having pried up a rock, Claudio swung it and caught the creature squarely in the face. It froze, and stared into him with its round eyes. Claudio heaved the stone straight on, through the creature's long beard and into its neck with a sickening crackle. The shaggy blue monster dropped to its knees, then slumped down dead.

They stood there a moment, staring.

Donna leaned over, extended a foot to cautiously nudge the creature, then recoiled when she noticed it had emptied its bladder. "What the F-Star *is* that thing?"

Falco hissed, "That kind of language disgraces the uniform."

"Well the uniform already disgraced *me*."

Still shaken, Claudio looked up at Falco. "...Captain? I...I killed it. What happens *now?*"

13

"Ensign, look out!" Donna shoved Claudio aside as another creature darted into the glade. This was smaller, and behind jagged patterns of blue paint, looked quite human, in leather briefs and shoulder-pads with straps crossing his chest. He landed on a low crouch, poised to spring upward at the first of the three strangers to move, one of his fists wrapped in a gleaming steel blade.

He saw the creature on the ground.

In a flash he was there on his knees by its side, brown dreadlocks streaming behind him, then billowing past his face. Blind to the surrounding strangers he put a hand to its chest, threw his head back and cried out, "Nooooooooooooooooooooo!" The sound rustled a drizzle of purple leaves from above and smutterflies from below, a swirling lilac cyclone of loss.

Blinking within the hurricane, Donna looked at the Captain, "I think we killed his...pet. Yeti."

With barely a sound, a similar small humanoid flashed into view, darting between the monster and visitors, poised low to strike. "Raydo, I heard you lamenting. Was it...cosmic *irony?*" This was a girl's voice.

The hunter stood, his eyes dragging against the weight of the dead monster. Finally he looked up at his companion and coldly intoned, "These intruders must die."

Her eyes and teeth glinted in a smile as her long, limber arm curled a blade into position, "Just don't tell me they must die *pretty.*" She rose to his side and gently punched his shoulder with a quick, low laugh.

Raydo pointed his expressionless face at

Claudio. "This one's mine."

Suddenly Claudio found himself in a blur with four limbs coming at him in rapid succession. He blocked the ones he could, trying to keep track of which one held the blade, and took several punishing strokes from the other three.

"Only two for Zayger? I'll *race* you," the girl tried to snarl toughly but her smile was irrepressible. Her blade flashed within an inch of Falco's nose before Donna could insert herself between them, and once more she nudged and jostled the Captain back while fending off the series of lightning strikes and swings from Zayger.

"*Damnit* Lieutenant – *get out of my way!*"

Claudio's stomach siezed up in frustration as he struggled to fend off the swarm of blows and swipes from the low, blurry creature. Accepting three hits and a stinging slash across the cheek he gathered himself for a single punch. But before he could swing he saw his own feet in the air, swept from beneath him, and the ground pounded against his back as he landed.

Pouncing to pin Claudio down, Raydo raised the blade, and cracked a smile.

Falco once again tried to shove past Donna, "Look, he didn't mean to kill your-- What the F-star *is* this thing?"

♭

"That," a syllable sent a wave through the glade "is the Bollox." The feminine voice was at once airy like a rustle of leaves and heavy like a waterfall, its tone vibrated the forest from the treetops to the soil. The hunters snapped to attention, the space-travelers felt a strange wave of warmth in their midsections.

Majestically she stepped into the clearing, tall and broad and fearless. Her orange-yellow hair cascaded in a mane of ringlets, framing her wide cheekbones and dimpled chin. Large blue-green eyes peered out from under thick, sandy brows. A leather corset emphasized her hourglass figure of powerful shoulders, wide hips and muscular thighs. Her broad, full breasts were proudly defiant of clothing and gravity.

She was solid as a tree-trunk, and yet a curious breeze could play with the various chiming blue beads in her hair, dangling from her clothing, and hanging in loose bracelets round her wrists and ankles.

Falco felt a gnawing in the pit of his stomach.

ᛚ

"Raydo. Zayger. Here," she commanded.

The hunters sulked to her sides, Raydo mumbling "This *can't be* right."

"Right is forever revealing itself," she said calmly, and the travelers realized that these hunters were teenagers, now dwarfed by a full adult.

Falco stepped forward, "And I thank *you* for revealing...*your*self. And what do you like to be called? And what would you like to be called...by *me?*"

"Bayla, priestess of Deia, and this is Shayra, my apprentice." She was accompanied by a smaller, darker version of herself. The girl nodded. "Raydo and Zayger, two of our hunters."

"I am Calvin Falco, captain of the Interstellar Syndication Starship Exogamy. Lieutenant Donna Trankh and ensign..." realizing he'd forgotten, Falco mumbled, "Che Guevara..."

"Claudio Rivera."

"Yes," Falco said, "Take us to your leader, he and I have arrangements to make. Tell him I bring valuable, um..." he patted down his pockets, "...ah, irresistible breath mints..?"

The apprentice raised her palms, "If you're looking for Kayno he has joined the chorus of spirits."

"Then tell him the Hidden Valley yodeling champion has *arrived*," Falco declared.

Donna nudged him, "I think she means he's dead, Captain."

Flicking a mint into his mouth, Falco stepped toward the priestess, "Well as a Syndicate captain, allow me to offer my services in the transition, or fulfillment of the position. Or any other services or positions you deem...fulfilling."

Wide-eyed, Claudio whispered to Donna, "Wow – it's like reading one of his stories."

"You mean the corny dialogue? Or the slutty aliens?"

ƀ

"The successor is already revealed," the priestess said, advancing toward Claudio and laying a finger on his chest, "The Bollox has chosen. You."

"...What?" Falco squinted.

"Tonight the mighty Bollox gives its flesh and

blood to strengthen us and sanctify the ground. And upon you it bestows its most private parts to imbibe, and thus be imbued with the fortitude of leadership."

Falco shook his head, *"What?"*

Claudio stepped back from her finger, "Wait - imbibe on its *what?*"

"This man can't be your king. Assuming political position is against regulation."

Donna hissed, "Captain, you *never* think about regulation before assuming a position."

"Lieutenant."

"You can't stand that this pornographic priestess chose the ensign over you."

The apprentice stepped forward, "The Bollox chose him. With its final glorious charge."

Falco thought a moment, then quickly swiped up the stone from the ground and threw it at the monster's head. "It moved. Did everyone else see it move just now? It wasn't fully dead before. You saw it charge, correct?"

Claudio's mouth gaped, "Captain, I..."

"Ensign."

"Enjoy your dinner, Captain." the ensign saluted.

Falco nodded, then swiveled to face the priestess, "Now please. Lead us to your village, I will imbue myself and demonstrate my fortitude in any way you require."

ß

Having politely tolerated this scene, Bayla the priestess resumed the business at hand. "Raydo, Zayger, bring the Bollox to the stream and have those hunters begin preparing it."

Flashing resentful glances the teenagers grasped the creature's shoulders and sulked it off past the edge of the glade. Watching them go, Claudio noticed for the first time that the brush at the clearing's edge now contained a mix of men, peering in with the same blue face-paint. As the teenagers passed, the hunters receded back into the forest.

"As for the village," Bayla turned back to the visitors, "it's on its way here."

"What, right *here?*"

The apprentice sniffed around and smiled with approval, "Our new sanctuary, the world navel at the end of a happy trail. Center of our village this next thirteen moons."

Falco caught himself mid-laugh, then captained up again, "Excuse me, little girl, I'm talking to your mother."

The priestess's green eyes flashed with annoyance. "Shayra is my apprentice, and she knows how to speak."

"But how can you pick your campsite so randomly?"

"We didn't," Shayra chimed, "The Bollox has chosen it. Wisely."

"Yes of course, the Bollox again," Falco sneered, "how could I have been so stupid?"

"I don't know. You appear healthy and intelligent."

"But you can't possibly trust this hungry monster to dictate your policies."

"...You don't have hungry monsters to dictate policy?" the apprentice peered curiously.

"No, we have billionaires, brokers and

bureaucrats with spreadsheets and stock-folders."

"These creatures sound terrifying. Are they the reason you abandoned your home?"

"We didn't abandon our home. They send us out to establish friendly relations, mutually satisfying planetary intercourse and exchange. *You* abandoned your home to follow some ridiculous animal."

"The soil around our old sanctuary was getting tired, so the Bollox led us to this bountiful place. Here we can be friendly without stocks and brokers. We mutually exchange with the forest, and all are provided for."

"What a load of crap," Falco muttered.

Shayra reached into a pouch hanging from her belt, "Yes, if you need to make a load of crap, Deia will appreciate it. Here." She handed him some seeds.

"Do you...wipe yourselves...with these?"

"No, they're hungberry seeds – if you put them in your load of crap we'll have berries growing here."

"I don't need to... Forget it." Falco tossed the seeds over his shoulder.

ᛒ

"Raise him." the priestess said as the hunters returned and handed her a satchel.

The young hunter advanced toward the ensign, but snapped back, "This-- *Whatever*-it-is, can't be Kayno. The Bollox--"

"Ran from you and chose someone else."

"Got confused by these ugly aliens in these ridiculous costumes--"

"If you cannot live by our laws then go make your own laws in the desert."

"Fine," the teenager grunted. "Deia knows I'm right. Come on, Zayger."

The huntress sputtered hesitantly, "I-- She-- He--"

"*Raydo,*" the apprentice whispered, drawing his eyes to hers, "Every dream will have its moon."

"Raise him," Bayla said again.

Zayger the huntress clamped Claudio's ankles and pulled. His arms wheeled as he fell backward but Raydo caught his wrists and he hung suspended between the teenagers. The priestess wrapped a sash of blue fur around his waist while her apprentice fitted him with leather shoulder-pads.

"Captain..?" he squeaked.

"Play along, ensign. This situation may yet yield some fascinating angles for...observation."

Donna leaned toward him, "Have you observed that these aliens have eyes in their *heads?* And not on their fannies? Captain?"

The priestesses were squatting, tying on his leather bracelets and furry ankle-bands.

"I am observing Syndicate proposition three seventy-four, 'a captain's duty to thoroughly survey *all* precious natural resources. And probe at discretion.'"

"Stand him," the priestess commanded, then applied the final touch: a headband with two short horns sticking out, "May Kayno be forever young, eternally virile. May he, like the mighty Bollox be ever wily, and like the rolling sky be ever constant. May Kayno put others first and his own satisfaction last." She raised her palms and nodded, "Here we are."

"Here we are," the apprentice and hunters responded.

"This is, um..." Claudio looked down at the wristbands and sash, "Captain?"

Falco smirked, "Yes, I'll tell Santa you're ready to join in the reindeer-games."

The young hunter hissed, "Even your almighty 'Santa' won't be able to save you from--"

"Raydo." the priestess intoned sternly, "They need help pitching tents over there."

The boy spat, swished his dreadlocks and lumbered away.

ᛟ

Shayra the apprentice walked a curious circle around Donna, sniffing and peering at her tattered uniform. "Your strange clothing is neither useful nor dignified...so what *is* it supposed to do?"

"This is a wardrobe malfunction – what's *your* excuse?"

"We don't need an excuse to look good," the priestess said, "The spirits don't want us to hide in shame."

"But don't you ever want to stand up for yourselves? Tell these men you want to dress with some dignity?"

"We *do* dress with dignity. And we expect our men to *deal* with it. Shayra, take her to Ayma's tent," the priestess said, "she'll have some old clothes."

Donna glanced a plea at Falco. He looked her down and up, and nodded his assent. The apprentice led her away into the wood.

Meanwhile the priestess had begun her examination of Claudio.

"Look, I appreciate the..." he cleared his throat, "it's a nice rack, but--"

"Thank you. And your antlers are majestic," she said, examining his palms.

"But I'm not a leader, I couldn't afford one semester of officer training."

"Take a slow deep breath," she put an ear to his chest.

"And the Syndicate's most famous captain, Calvin Theseus Falco is standing *right here*."

"He may be, but the Bollox chose *you*. Open your mouth." She pried his jaw to check his teeth and tongue, he warbled a protest and she responded, "It's never been wrong in seeing the Kayno we need."

"It saw *him*, I just got in the way because I've been trained to get myself killed."

"And when we eat tonight the Bollox will become part of you, your monster spirit-guide."

"But if you need a man who's guided by his bollocks--"

"Not only the spirit of the Bollox, but the spirits of the trees, the rocks and streams, the spirits of our ancestors, they will fill your body, guide your way. The skin of Kayno is a suit the spirits wear, their strength will guide your bones and muscle. You'll manifest their will, to protect us." Satisfied with the exam, she leaned in and tugged his collar to take a long inhale of his scent. "Yes, you're the one. Zayger. Take him to Ayma's tent. She'll want to sniff and poke at him before the ritual."

The huntress nimbly approached and took a quick sniff for herself, grinned bashfully at Bayla and snatched Claudio's wrist. "It'll be alright. Take some deep breaths before you meet her and try not to inhale when she's near." Then she jerked him like a rag-doll and darted from the glade, trailing his body and flailing limbs, his eyes still grasping for the Captain as he disappeared into the rustling brush.

ᛉ

Falco assumed one of his statue poses – heroic and scholarly "He might understand if he'd ever felt the rush of command--"

The priestess smiled benevolently. "You do not understand what we need here."

"*Make* me understand." He dug his heels into the moss.

"We don't need some big dictator."

"You only say that because you don't know *how* big. Wait, did you say--"

"Our guardian spirits choose someone to *protect us* from domination, keep us in balance."

"*Balance?* Following some brainless space-monster from campsite to campsite – you're going nowhere!"

"And you assume we long to become like the ship you steered into destruction?"

Falco snuffed quizzically, "What...makes you think..?"

"Is *that* your ship, the Exogamy you're so proud of?"

"No, that's a pathetic jettison-pod." Realizing that they were being observed by curious villagers, the Captain adjusted his volume to full oratory. "The Exogamy was the pride of the fleet, sleek, beautiful and deadly. If she were above us, you'd all fall to your knees in wonder like the hundred other tribes we've enlightened and civilized. They write hymns *and limericks* about Captain Falco. You *need me*. *Because* I'm guided by my bollocks – instinct and ambition, *that's* how things get done."

Bayla circled him, eyeing his sculpted body, the princely curve of his back, the clench of his calves, the proud shelf of his abdomen. She ran her fingertips down his chest, then curiously dipped a finger into his clavicle. "...What a marvel you are..."

"Lots of planets have females and males. But you're looking at a real *man*."

The dank surrounding underbrush hungrily rustled as Deian observers leaned in, breathlessly.

♭

"I imagine you're a rare specimen even among your own people." She stared straight and deep into his eyes and he realized for the first time she was just a little bit taller than him.

"Only eight other captains have starships like mine. And I've beaten them *all* at poker *and*...ping-pong. Some of your customs may at first appear idiotic but I'm a fast learner."

"You're a champion."

"With sword, pen, *and*...castanets." A soft thud nearby, someone had swooned. "*Tell me* I'm not more attractive than him."

"But you *are* more attractive than him."

"What..? Then why are we negotiating? We

could be ruling this planet, you and I."

A pause. Then she doubled over with musical laughter, underscored by the jangle of dangling beads. "*You* could rule Deia!"

"*We*, I said *we--*" That glimpse of her teeth – broad and strong with a gap in the middle.

"Captain bollocks is going to tell Deia what to do!"

"Captain *Falco*."

"What planet are you from, Falco?"

"Earth."

"And is she obedient to the will of real *men* like you? Satisfy your every ambition, this Earth? And do you boldly trek the stars to teach natives how to spank their worlds into submission? Or have your advances on Earth been rejected, and you've gone to take out your frustration on other planets?"

"Earth? She can't get enough of *real man*. But my people dream *bigger*. We're the human race, no single planet could limit our ambition."

"So you penetrate the skies with your steely vessel, thrusting through the cosmos to spread seeds of your culture."

"That's...not the *exact* wording of the captain's oath. But I might recommend a revision."

The priestess reddened sternly, green eyes darting. "Everybody *back,*" her voice shook the trees.

Over his shoulder, Falco saw a flurry of limbs, women who'd been reaching from behind him, scurried and scampered back toward the village.

"Your needs and ambition drag you across the galaxy, far from your home. And you dragged your crew to their death. And here you are, little Calvin without a scratch, ready to steer this tribe on a world you've never seen."

"That's *Captain* little-- I meant--"

"*Are* you a captain? With no ship? And a crew of two?"

"Well what the hell are *you*? Look at yourself!"

"Yes, let's *both* stare at my body, Calvin."

"Some kind of priestess you say - the slimiest brothels in the galaxy have more modesty."

"How fascinating – please tell me more about the slimiest brothels."

Falco sullenly bit his bottom lip. "Fine, that was stupid. You've got my mind all twisted up. You're...the most delightful creature I've ever seen..."

"Thank you but that does not answer my question. *Are* you still a captain?"

"Yes I am. I earned these stripes. I get more press than any man in the fleet and I've written over a hundred and *three* published stories." He reached into his belt-pack, "I could buy your whole planet on royalties from Captain Falco the action figure."

"What an adorable little...plastic god..."

"It's not a god, it's *me*. With my *old* hairstyle. Press the button, it talks."

"You're...the most delightful creature I've ever seen..." it said.

"Forget it said that, press it again."

"No, I wouldn't want to smudge your...shiny little ego. Calvin." She handed back the figure.

"Yeah, I get it. Call me whatever you want."

"Can we be friends?"

"Wow... 'Just friends.' Back at the academy we used to call that 'the Platonic Bomb.' I'd *heard* about it but never... *Never...*"

"Think about it. You're welcome here as a friend, but neither this tribe nor I have any need of a captain. You'll excuse me, I've got arrangements to make." She smiled warmly and blushed, he melted a little bit inside, "I'm getting married."

He watched her bound off like a gazelle. Through the leaves and fronds he could see activity, women assembling skeletal frames and leather-topped huts that humped like pregnant bellies from the ground. Hunters were assembling wooden racks, some were already built and hung with prey-animals. Someone started drumming and village voices coalesced into a calming mid-tempo worksong. Falco stalked off into the fragrant forest to take a leak.

ᛉ

Zayger, the little huntress, sat down at the edge of the glade and Claudio sat down beside her, wiping his face with a handkerchief. He watched her carefully select several strands of grass and slip them from their sheaves, then intently tie them together.

"So Ayma is your...what? Town pot-head? Witchdoctor?"

The girl's attention remained on the knot in her hand, "She is the waning moonshiner, listener of the spirits." Zayger looked over at him. "She hears Kayno in you."

"I don't claim a broad understanding of

women, but she slapped me repeatedly and broke raw *eggs* on my face. *I* would interpret that more like she *doesn't* approve."

Zayger grinned, her sharp teeth glinting. "It's true you don't know women. If she disapproved she never would have wasted the eggs." Then her smile burst into a giggle and she punched Claudio's arm.

"Ow. But you don't...*really* believe this monster can tell who has the wisdom to rule a community..?"

"Ha! That sounds very stupid," she said, casting a lasso of tied grass onto a patch of blue moss and staring at it. "The Bollox will fight the man most like a Bollox. And that's the one we need. But Kayno doesn't *rule* anyone except Kayno, his needy, greedy animal self. When the ancient Bollox tried to rule the forest he only made a magnificent fool of himself. And he's been a fugitive running ever since. What we need... When a strong hunter can control his *own* Bollox, the hidden Bollox inside, then we respect him and follow his example."

"So tonight, the rave, I'll eat the...um..?"

"The bowl of Bollox bollocks." She jerked the string, and caught something small and fuzzy in her hand.

"Yes, and then hear a story, followed by a...dance?"

"You'll dance the part of Deio, sky-father and Bayla will be Deia the ground-mother. Your dance will assure abundant rain in the coming year, fertilize the land." It was some sort of caterpillar.

"Yes, but about the dancing part... Could you show me the steps?"

She laughed again and punched his arm, "Ha!

No, when the priestess leads, Kayno will know his part."

A male voice from behind said "I'll assume you've told him that if he fails, he's clearly *not* Kayno and we'll tear him to pieces."

Zayger looked at Raydo, then back at Claudio. "...Did I?"

"...Zayger?" Claudio's eyes widened. She hadn't.

"Naturally if Deio was offended or bored the skies would clench. Without rain our crops would wither. Then we'd need to remind him of rain by spraying the camp with your blood."

"And you *won't show me* how to do this dance?"

Raydo howled with laughter, but Zayger shrugged, "A bollox-beater won't fail."

"Except Trayner," Raydo said.

"Oh yeah, Trayner," Zayger laughed, "but that was just ridiculous, he didn't know *what* to do. It was like he came from a different *planet.*"

"Good crops though, once we'd watered the fields with him."

Claudio blurted, *"I'm* from a different planet! Zayger, are you going to--"

"I'll show you how to dance." Raydo beckoned with a malevolent grin.

"Don't dance with Raydo."

Claudio launched to his feet and squared his chest at Raydo. "*This* is a dance I know. You think you know me?"

"I see through your metal pod and fancy clothes, I see a mucklucking suck-worm looking for something healthy to latch onto."

Claudio advanced on the teenager, "You want to know what's under this uniform? A kid from Newark. Then five years of internment camp before joining the syndicate. You think I don't know tough guys muscling around, trying to be tribal chieftains? I've been *all my life* around punks like you and *none* of em's ever held me down. You wanna test me? Choose any weapon. *I choose these hands.*"

Raydo stared him down hard. Then threw back his head, rustling his dreadlocks with a laugh. "I'll face exile for murdering *you?* Why, when I can happily join in your public execution? Because you *will* fail. Tonight, tomorrow, next moon? You will expose your weakness and we will all tear you apart." The young man leaned closer to confide, "And I will keep your hands. Tied to my belt. And every time I scratch myself with them I will hope your spirit is around to see." Then he walked off into the forest.

Zayger released the caterpillar and watched it scrunch away. "Raydo is a good guy, don't worry. He'll get tired of your severed hands, eventually, let the gardeners plant them with the other chunks of your mangled body."

"Speaking of..." Claudio's lips pursed as he considered a moment. "Zayger. Of all the women in the village, you're the only one dressed like a..."

"A hunter. I've always been a hunter. As a child I said I'll be a hunter with this tribe or alone in the desert. So at thirteen I took the hunter's trials and earned a hunter's name. And if anybody says you can't be a hunter without balls?" She flashed her knife, "I'll let them know how it feels."

Again she laughed and punched him, but this time he gently deflected it, "In my culture there are 'hunters' who can laugh without punching each other."

"Yes, a *strange* world..."

ᛒ

"You come from a camp," the huntress continued, "but different from this. What was it like?"

"I was born in a toxic swamp called Amurrica, twelve years old when my father took me south to enlist in the Syndicate. Wading through miles of waste until we reached the border-fence of Brazil. We could see the space-ports, the academy, Santa's animatronic village. But like all other refugees we were locked in the internment camps."

"I was in-turd once, it doesn't wash off so easy."

"In that cage you learn to look out for each other. Your only chance of survival is to make sure everybody gets their share. So they won't kill you in your sleep. I guess when the electronic eyes see you're willing to go hungry, they know you're ready to die for the Syndicate."

"And the Syndicate is...Santa?"

Claudio laughed. "In a way, I guess. Magical sleds, bags of toys, unpaid elf-labor? But it's the anti-Santa for planets we discover."

"Doesn't your planet have a mother? Like Deia?"

"Maybe it did, once, I guess the sky-father divorced her or something. Became angry, jealous, throwing dead souls in a refugee camp called Purgatorio. Finally we scrapped all that, it was his lieutenants we really liked, Santa Claus and the Easter Bunny. They watch us all the time but they don't really care what we do, they give us stuff anyway. And if you're scared of what happens after death there's an old code-word, you say 'John...three-one-six?' Six-one-three? One of those, right before you die and you transport to someplace called Sugar-Candy Mountain."

"What's it like?"

"I hear it smells much better than the swamps and the camps. Fruit trees, clean water... I guess it's a lot like here."

Just then the huntress tensed up and stood, swiveling to face Donna and the apprentice as they entered the clearing. Donna was now wearing a leather corset, with the remains of her syndicate button-down cut to a short jacket. Zayger grinned and blushed.

Shayra the apprentice took Claudio's hand and pulled him to his feet. "I'll help you with your face-paint," she said and walked him away. Zayger followed, but seeing Falco step into the glade she stopped and crouched in the brush to watch them in secret.

ᛉ

"Lieutenant," Falco surveyed her new outfit.

"Captain," she stood stiffly.

"You look..."

"I know it's against regulation to alter a uniform, but this came out of *my* salary, it's--"

"Lovely. You look lovely, lieutenant."

"Thank you," she grinned, relaxing her posture.

Zayger leaned and snapped a twig but they ignored her.

"Tell me what you've learned about the Deians."

"About a hundred and eighty people. The men hunt, women grow a little patch of what look like corn, squash and beans. Everything is shared."

"Space-communists."

"More like space socialists."

"And who's the grand Kommissar?"

"There's a very old medicine woman called Ayma, had to be carried here, the former high priestess. She sits by her tent, smoking a pipe, hears voices, supposedly from the forest spirits and the dead."

"A pot-head witch-doctor... Perfect."

"But it's the spirits. They speak through the old woman, the high priestess and the apprentice, they're like the triple-form of Deia their goddess. The girl is really nice, Shayra, she gave me materials to build a tent. For us..?"

Falco cocked an eyebrow. "'Us'?"

"We might be here a while, and... Calvin..."

"*Captain*."

"Captain... Our pod didn't crash on one of the planets entirely covered in snow, or sand or lava. We're not melting in the garbage-marshes of New New Jersey. By total random chance we're not in a holding cell in any of the sectors where you have unpaid parking tickets or paternity suits. Out of all endless space, we're in this enchanted forest with these friendly creatures...and they speak *English!* What are the odds of *that?* And they seem happy and...I think we could be happy too... You could hunt, I could garden, we could...live in a little tent?"

ß

Falco leaned in and jutted his jaw, "We're not tourists on some hippie honeymoon. I'm a captain, you're an officer."

"There's nothing in regulation against it. Actually Syndicate proposition sixty nine says a captain can proposition anyone in the Syndicate."

"I believe you mean proposition six nine*teen* and I'm well aware of it. But I say a captain should be equally accountable to every member of the crew. Falco doesn't play favorites."

"'*Favorites?*' Between me and *who?* There *is* no crew. Ensign Rivera is getting his face painted, he's about to eat monster-balls and get possessed by forest spirits. There's you and me..." She breathed in tentatively, her big dark eyes shining. Then she relaxed her lids and said in a sultry voice, "I remember a night, out of uniform...taking turns as the Easter bunny...

The Captain snapped, "Is that *all* you can think about? I have needs too."

"Right," she turned cold, "Like you *need* to desecrate that extraterrestrial so you can write *another* Starbuck magazine story."

"What I *need* right now is a *lieutenant.* Damnit what I *really* need is a fembot. Then we could civilize these savages *and* make it like battery-rabbits."

"You could...pretend I'm a fembot..?"

"Pretend you're a fembot so I could *pretend* I'm pretending you're a woman? 'Never work – any mention of sex would give me a splitting headache."

A rustle and thud in the brush let them know Zayger had leaned too far and fallen down. They ignored it.

"Captain, the ship was destroyed, we got clobbered in that pod, I hit my head, I got hit by *your* head, I feel all scrambled up and... And I just don't know if that's who I really am..."

"*Lieutenant.*"

"Fine. You need a lieutenant? Then as your navigator I have a right to know *why* you plunged us into that asteroid field. Bearing toward forbidden airspace near an enemy colony. Was it suicide? Is that why you fired and replaced all your classic officers last month?"

"And as a captain I have a right to say *cool your jets.*"

"Or was it personal? Everybody knows your old academy sweetheart is living there with Colonel Whambam since defecting from the Syndicate. Were we about to start World War Nine? Over your ex-girlfriend?"

"..? *Magellen?* She wasn't worth the *last* World War we started over her. She's not even a real brunette. And the uni-brow? Implants."

"Captain, you're...taking evasive action... Oh my stars... We weren't on a mission... You got all those people killed... Two hundred crew-members..."

"There were only thirty crew-members. The rest were all quality consultants, they won't be missed. And of *course* we were on a mission – if you think I'd recklessly endanger my crew, at *least* I'd expect you to know I wouldn't endanger my *ship* without..."

"Without *what? What was the mission?*"

"I think you deserve to know..."

"...So?"

"But it's classified above lieutenant."

Donna froze a moment, a statue of shock and frustration. Then a hand slapped the Captain so hard he reeled and fell, and before she could figure out who to defend him from, Donna realized the hand was hers.

With a dancer's leap to his feet again, Falco grinned darkly.

"Is *that* how you like it, Captain?" Donna swiveled and stalked away.

Falco nodded at her hips. Like a space-minx.

♭

Then Falco felt a hand pat him on the back. *"Women,"* said the little huntress.

"Oh, *great.*"

"They never shut up in *your* world either? About the things you *didn't even* say? Eh?"

Falco silenced her with a blue stare of frosty boredom. Then he sighed. "Well I'm glad we had this little talk. Best of luck to you, young...whatever."

"Wait! Calpitan."

"Call me... Forget it."

"You gave her the cold boner."

"What?"

Zayger sputtered, "If she tried to put her

head-- on your collar-bone-- you-- would be cold..."

"...Thanks..."

"The cold boner!" Zayger laughed and punched his arm.

"*Hey.* My personal space...will be the *final frontier for your hand* if you put it on me again."

"I'm sorry – wait!"

"What? What do you want?"

"I've never seen someone act like you. You're like a giant skrote. The way they charge forward with their furry chest out and a gungan egg under one arm. You've hunted skrote, right?"

"Wrong."

"They're vicious. But they taste great and you get to keep the egg? Make a sauce with it. Anyway, charging across the field, chased by a stampede, jowns to the left, cloakers to the right, the skrote with his little horns cocked for impact - like *you*. Like the world and all the stars are yours, and everyone and everything is too stupid to know it. I want to *be* a... I want to be like you."

"No. Absolutely not."

"Calpitan."

"No. Because *every time* some kid says he wants to be like me? Gets himself killed and then *I* have to look somber for the rest of the mission. Even though I always *love* the rest of the mission."

"You said you need a helper. I know this forest. I can help you. Calpitan."

"Look, my *name* is..." Falco sighed, "Call me Captain."

"Captain. CAPTAAAAAAIN!" she shouted, overjoyed, "I...*really* want to punch your arm right now."

"You're *really* making the smart choice. Not doing it. I don't need a helper who's crippled."

"Can I...fan it? Or something?"

"No, I don't need a fan either. Look, put 'er there."

"I'll get her. Who?"

"Your hand. No, your other hand. This is called a shake. Then you do a swish with the ship and...boom."

"Boom...*Wow.* So the ship explodes... Your hand is a ship?"

"No, the ship drops a bomb, the *planet* explodes, it was a deadbeat planet, your hand becomes the... We'll work on it some more later."

"We *will.* I will *be* the ship and the planet and the explosion. Let's do it again right now."

"Right now I need to get some seed-bars from the pod."

"I'll be your lookout. Then we'll shake."

"*No.* Act normal. Whatever that is. Go around and punch your friends – when I need your help I'll ask."

"And we'll *shake.*"

"Yes, we'll shake. Now run along."

"Wait, just... Please."

"Alright, fine." They shook again. "Boom."

"BOOM!"

"Good. You can learn."

"Zayger *learns.* I get totally *schooled.* You'll see. I am a booger on your thumb, ready to be flicked across the *sky!* Zayger away!" She galloped off into the woods. Falco sighed and lightly touched his forehead. Then he walked to the pod.

ƺ

Afternoon passed and the village was completed, a circle of round leather huts. They looked like pink mushroom caps half-emerged from the ground, a ship flying overhead could have mistaken them for part of the flora. Small, merry parties of women gathered roots and fungus. Blindfolded children bounded over each other in a circle, laughing.

The village firekeeper had been last to arrive, gently carrying a primitive bird-cage-looking contraption, to light the central blaze. Songs were sung, hands were held, then mothers carried small torches to their huts.

Hunters reverently entered the glade and set a ring of torches at the perimeter.

Raydo carried a wooden table into the clearing. It wasn't heavy, but he could hear light footsteps behind him with a slight girlish spring and the light bustle of beads. Knowing it was Shayra, he decided to look tired and sullen. Setting the table down, he leaned on it heavily, letting his long brown dreadlocks roll across his shoulderblades and fall over his face.

A tray of food gently touched down on the table. The smell of it made him feel warm and happy, it was festival soup. But with a struggle he managed to maintain his stony demeanor.

"Raydo," he could hear her posture in her voice, the hand on her hip.

"What?"

"You're not looking at me. *More* than usual." He could hear the raised eyebrow.

"I'm busy."

"You're cranky. Raydo, I... I've had a vision. Of your future. Do you want to hear it?"

The hunter's eyes desperately searched. For *anything*, anything except her. One of the torches had a loose knot. He walked over to fix it, "Not unless I'm Kayno and you're--"

"No you're not Kayno," he heard the sprightly jingle approaching from behind, "But you *are* wearing a crown!" And she flipped a bowl of soup on his head, slimy, sloshing through his hair.

Reflexively he turned and whipped his dreadlocks around, splashing her. He couldn't open his eyes but could still see her leap behind the table, grab a fistfull of seeds from a bowl and spray them at him.

"Stop it, I don't want to play!" He launched himself across, hearing her giggle reminded him of his anger and he shoved at her shoulders. But she brushed his hands outward and bumped his foreheard with hers. The giggling again as he staggered backward, hands flailing as his body began to fall. She clasped his hands and pulled him hard again, this time pounding his abdomen with her chest. Then her fingers gripped his lower ribs and he stopped.

Raydo blinked the soup from his eyes. Shayra's face, so close, it filled his field of vision, the wild, curly black hair. Her dark brown eyes and thick, brushy brows. Her broad round cheeks and tiny chin. Her guord-shaped nose with wide nostrils like wings in glide. He'd known this face from their infancy, better than he knew his own. But suddenly he felt like he'd never seen her lips before. Ripe like berries ready to be plucked. Her face was getting closer. No, he realized *his* face was getting closer. And slowly tilting.

Then something hooked the back of his heel and the mossy ground slammed his shoulders.

She'd tripped him.

"That's not fair combat," he grumbled at the open sky above.

"That's why they only teach it to girls."

ƀ

Raydo sat up and wiped a slimy dreadlock from his shoulder. "And here we are again, wearing *another* festival soup. Shayra we're not supposed to be children anymore."

"Then *why* do they keep cooking extra soup every year?" She knelt behind him, wiping his hair. "And *you've* been acting like a child all day."

"*Who's* acting like a child? *You* were supposed to be priestess by now."

"It isn't time yet..."

"It's time when *you wake up* and realize what everybody knows – you're ready. We're all waiting for you. Ayma is waiting for permission to die, Bayla is waiting to take Ayma's place--"

"Raydo I had a vision last month in the cave. The forest weeping in flames, a swarming flock of black skowls, a cold killer with metallic eyes, a white man dancing... Something is coming, something our customs have not prepared us for... I don't know if anyone can save us, but I know I'm not ready."

The hunter's face twisted in anger. "It's these space creatures. *They're* the skowls, *they're* the hungry ghosts and the fire was their ship. Bayla can't see it but you can, and that's why we need you to lead us."

"I thought of it too when they first arrived, but now that I've listened to them... They're too stupid to pose any real danger. Like children in a wind-spitting contest."

"And now one of these children will be Kayno."

"Because the Bollox--"

"Because nobody has the stones to tell Bayla when she's wrong. Sometimes I feel like I could just-- Just--"

"*What* do you feel like doing with Bayla, that had you hunting the Bollox?"

"Ow."

"Hold still. This is knotted."

"Wait a minute. You think I was hunting the Bollox so I could become the priestess's pet?"

"Well?"

"I wasn't going to, but then I looked around at all the other hunters... Hayzer with his idiotic pranks, Laymo with his stupid jokes, Rayjer with his drinking problem, Gamer with his bone-dice. And then I thought of...our last Kayno..."

"I know..."

"And I asked myself... Who's gonna replace him? Who here is as wise, as strong? Who can break the wind as silently? And break the silence with laughter as loudly?"

"His...judicious ability...to frame bystanders for his flatulence will live on in legend..."

"And... And I'm not him, I know it, but I had to try... I didn't do it for myself, I really thought...I was doing the right thing for the tribe."

"You always do the right thing for the tribe. And the tribe...loves you...for it."

The hunter sighed. "We'd better go rinse off in the river."

"Only if you promise to stare. Then quickly turn when I look your way."

Raydo felt something in his belly, warm and bright, a smile. He clenched his jaw as he felt it rising through his chest and up his neck, he jerked his head to pull a dreadlock curtain across his face but it was all sticky. So he just beamed, heat in his cheeks, a cold breeze on his back teeth. But she was already marching toward the stream.

"Alright, I promise," he grumbled, and followed.

ʒ

Zayger grinned from the brush, watching them leave the glade. She entered with a replacement tray and began fixing the wreckage of the table. Then she froze, aware of the dusky scent and heavy presence behind her. With a majestic tolling of beads, the priestess strode into the glade.

"Zayger," she said.

Zayger resumed fixing the bowls, pretending she hadn't heard.

"Oh, Zayger?" Bayla sang out musically.

Zayger giggled but kept pretending.

"Zayger."

"Say 'Zayger' again."

"No. But as our keenest tracker and swiftest runner--"

"Also I just found out I can bend my finger back this far? I don't know *yet* how it will make me a better hunter, but--"

"You can read the tone of the forest creatures. What do you read in the village?"

Zayger beamed up at Bayla, teeth glinting. "A lot of curiosity about the new Kayno. When I led him to Ayma's tent the children stopped their blindfold bounce, wanted to touch his hair."

"Did he let them?"

"He got down and played an animal, they laughed like chatter-squawks. Several hunters have inquired if Donna-tennant is aware that she's available. The women unanimously propose we apply war-captive rules to the captain, stud him for new blood in the tribe."

"I'm sure we'll see a crop of handsome babies in the spring. And what do *you* think?"

Suddenly antsy, the young huntress fumbled for her thoughts. "I-- I-- Look, a unicorn!" And she darted, giggling, through the brush.

♭

Bayla pulled a leather pouch from her belt and, taking a deep breath, poured some dust into her upturned palm. She raised it close to her face and inhaled its scent. Then slowly, gracefully she turned three times in a circle, blowing the dust so it scattered to the ground.

Folding down, she knelt low and leaned forward, pressing the palms of her broad hands into the dirt. Humming a low tone, gentle but firm, she kneeded the dust into the soil and touched her forehead to it. Then she turned her body a bit, and repeated the mixing in the next direction.

Claudio stepped into the clearing and watched her. The connection between the large, muscular woman and the strong, fertile ground was like nothing in the swamps of his childhood, or academy textbooks or starship corridors, and yet it seemed somehow familiar. Then he realized he was staring, and not just with his eyes – his nose and mouth were just as wide. He straightened and tried to speak but a fingertip on his shoulder stopped him. Looking back he saw Zayger the huntress. She grinned and touched her knuckle to his arm.

When she'd completed the circle, Bayla tilted her broad jaw back, eyes still lightly closed, opened her arms and ended the ritual with "Here we are."

"Is that..." Claudio had to clear his dry throat, "how you dance?"

She rose. "That's how we mingle the dust of last year's sanctuary with the dust of this one. Now this glade is part of us and we are part of it."

"It's fascinating. Beautiful. All of this."

"Shouldn't it be?" Bayla smiled at him, green eyes shining, cheeks round with blue spirals. "We have to live in it."

"Yes, of course..."

"...Yes?"

"Listen, no matter how many times I... Look. If you need a leader, Mister Right has *literally* descended from above. But it's not me. It's the Captain."

"You really admire him."

"The first time I saw Captain Falco... I'd been on the ship two weeks and I was dispatched to transport an urgent Grappaccino to the bridge. In the elevator I practiced what I'd say to him, but it was all stupid fan-boy stuff, 'you're the coolest thing in space,' like that, stupid. The doors opened and... Red alert, our weapons were down, right engine out and we were surrounded by six Gregarian ships, locked to fire once they finished their long-winded monologues. Our bridge-crew was crying and confessing their secret crushes, the grogg peed on the floor and our squid-monster communications officer spontaneously went into labor. *Chaos.* ...But in the middle of all this, calm in the center of the galactic crap-storm, Calvin Theseus Falco. Instructed the pilot, 'put our left engine in warp two' and while we spun faster than light he ordered the kitchen, 'jettison the leftover fruitcake-discs.' A moment later we were breathing easy, the Gregarians were pummeled to space-dust and the Captain had delivered five healthy squidlings. Everything I'd ever thought of saying to him seemed so...insufficient... I handed him the coffee, he sniffed it and said 'there's an access panel, back wall of sector 49, you climb through central heating and get out on deck 16. 'Cut ninety seconds off your delivery, and keep the coffee hot.' All I could say was 'Yes sir' and he...*almost*...looked me in the eye...but then he was called away to settle a dispute between a two-headed Republicrat."

"That's quite a story," the priestess said. "Did you leave out the part where he said thank you?"

"No, I left out the part where I had to wipe up grogg-mess and gallons of inky squid afterbirth. Then babysit the squidlings, which got confusing because... Squillia named all five after the Captain."

♭

The priestess put a hand on his shoulder, which looked small in comparison. Claudio realized that somehow she could adjust her posture when he spoke, so that she appeared to be looking upward at him. But standing this close, she was quite a bit taller.

"I like this story," she said, "And it's even better with the parts you added after. Share it at the rave tonight, we'll call it... 'How Claudio delivered coffee, cleaned a mess and nurtured newborn squidlings.'"

Claudio pulled his shoulder away, "What..? But it's *not* a story about Claudio, me, *at all*. You're missing the point. I was a walk-on, a cameo, an extra in a story that should be called... 'Everyone was gonna *die*, but Captain Falco kept us alive *and* brought new squid-life into the galaxy.'"

"That's not the story I heard."

"But...we were surrounded by furious Gregarians."

"Right. Why were they furious?"

"Well the Gregarian queen...he invited her for a cup of coffee on the ship... But he *rescued us* while delivering squintuplets. What more could you want in a leader?

"Someone who would have allowed a pregnant crewmember to give birth in peace? Someone who would not have endangered the whole community by absconding with a queen in the first place?"

"Fine, he's not perfect. But he's never lost a fight."

"Because he's willing to endanger everyone around him. Especially the...'Extras'..? Here, no one is an 'extra.' Woven threads are stronger than single strands."

"I shouldn't have told you the story. Forget it."

"But you did and I loved it. Because one person did exactly what was needed, had the humility to learn, cleaned up messes while everyone else was making them. You're going to be a great Kayno."

"You're not listening to me." He tried to turn away.

She clamped his shoulders. "I *am* listening. And you're going to be a great Kayno."

"You're calmly repeating yourself regardless of what I tell you – *stop it*. I'm an adult. You can't talk me into this. Everyone here is under your spell. Fine. Your body looks like Thanksgiving? I get it. And I respect you. I respect this whole thing, this culture that revolves in orbit around your... Um."

"Around Deia."

"Around Deia, sorry. And because I respect you and...this... I can't be your Kayno or whatever."

"Each time you say that it proves you're the one."

"Don't touch me."

"And you're pretty when you're angry. Your eyes."

"*Back off.* I'm not gonna be mesmerized by your hypnotic orbs."

"Trust me."

"I can't think when you're so close."

"You'll learn," she said, gripped his shirt and

pulled him close so hard he had to reach with his toes to touch the ground. She whispered into his ear and he jerked away, glaring.

Claudio realized he was in a combat stance. But his limbs wouldn't move as she stepped into his space again, leaned in and whispered the rest.

She stepped back and stared into him. Upward, he realized, she'd adjusted her posture again.

"It's always been your destiny," her voice was breathy but calm.

His body remembered itself and launched him forward.

He took hold, as much of this woman as he could, with all his might. Pressing her firmly – how could she be so solid and yet so soft? Her eyes that had drilled into his were now inviting, deep, cavernous. He kissed her.

From every side, an erruption of chirping birds. No, chirping villagers, ringed around the clearing, surrounding them. The ceremony was about to begin.

ƻ

Drawn into the circle of spectators, Donna, the Syndicate navigator, scanned from face to face, lean men painted with blue triangles, broad women with spirals, round children with tadpole squiggles, all eyes fixed on Bayla and Claudio. So many faces, but there was one face she could not find.

Her eyes swept again from chin to chin: knob chin, cleft chin, wide chin, pointed chin, all types in rapid succession till she'd peered all around the circle and stopped – the chin right next to her. The perfect one. The chin you could sharpen a razor on. The long nose with its ever-so-slight hawk curve, the eagle brow. Somehow he'd appeared beside her. Captain Falco.

His face turned, she looked into his mood-stone eyes, now warm green.

"Lieutenant. I'm..."

"Sorry?" she burst out, "*Now* you're sorry? Everybody duck-and-cover, the fabric of space-time might tear asunder – Captain Falco is sorry!"

"What? No, I was gonna say I'm a little bit *itchy*. But if *you* don't want to scratch my back--"

"Wait!" she yelped.

"No, it's too late, forget it," he pulled the action figure from his belt and scratching his back with its boots. "Ahh. Someone I can *trust*."

"*That's* your problem – you treat women like objects and objects like women!"

Falco paused and shifted his brow in contemplation. Then he inquired, "How is that *my* problem?"

She didn't know what to say but was going to say it anyway, when a sudden silence descended on the crowd.

♭

A creature shuffled into the glade, accompanied by the low tolling of heavy beads. It looked like a living mushroom with long viney tendrils hanging and trailing behind. Then with low reverence each voice whispered "Ayma." It was the old woman in a low hood.

Without raising her head or showing her face, she spoke. "Welcome children of Deia. The bountiful one has brought us to a new year in a new home. And as further signs of her blessing, she delivers new faces. Among them the Bollox-beater, new skin of Kayno." Bayla opened her hands in a graceful blossoming motion toward Claudio, and watched the faces, each one nodding with a low "Hm."

Two more faces popped into the circle, Shayra and Raydo, still glistening from the stream and Bayla smiled at them. Ayma continued, "Tonight with the sacred blood we will water the field of our next harvest. And the Bollox will grant us its strength, so we become one flesh. But first we hear new voices. Shayra?"

The apprentice entered the circle and carefully lifted a flower-bulb from the table. Stepping toward Falco, she pointed the bulb at his chin.

Falco shrugged, "None for me, thanks, I brought a seed-bar."

She pulled the stem and it popped, a small puff of pollen.

Surprised, Falco adjusted his balance. Then his eyes widened. "Everything smells...blue...sunshine... Great Bowie's Ghost!" he gasped, peering around in alarm, "*Trees* are *alive*. I heard it but I never *believed* it... We're surrounded!"

Ayma approached, sternly. "Who are you?"

"Shhh! They can't smell us if we don't move."

"Who are you?"

Confused, Falco raised a hand in front of his face. It was holding a seed-bar. He stared at it.

"Captain...crunch..."

"Breathe. Who are you?"

"What?" Falco put the seed-bar to his ear, *"You're* alive? What do we *do?* ...What? But what would the *Syndicate..?* ...Yes. *Yes! Engage!"* And he sprinted off, grabbing a torch as he burst through the brush.

They watched the flame, darting and flickering as he disappeared into the darkening wood.

Zayger stepped forward, "I follow him?"

Ayma held up a hand. "We complete the ritual."

Shayra popped a second bulb toward Donna's face.

The old woman slumped over to her. "Who are you?"

Donna's eyebrow twitched, "I... Oh my stars... I don't... Captain!" And she bounded off after him.

♭

"I *have* to go," Claudio declared, but just then a puff of flower dust was popped toward his face as well. It smelled like lightning tapping a circle of drum-pads. It felt sweet, he blinked and saw flashes of perfume and slither.

He heard Bayla's hand on his chest and felt Ayma's voice "Who are you?"

His ears finally adjusted to hear a sound, it was his own voice mechanically babbling "Interstellar Syndicate ensign forty-two eleven dot four Rivera Claudio. Ensign swears to protect the captain, ship and all other Syndicate properties, though it may entail gruesome death in manners including but not limited to incineration, mastication, defenestration, vaporization, depilitation, recitation--"

"*Who are you?*"

"Isolation, exploitation, mutilation... Mutation... Wait, I think I'm getting confused. Interstellar Syndicate ensign forty-two eleven dot four--"

Ayma pressed her open hand to his face, "*Who are you?*"

Claudio found himself alone, in the darkness. "I...don't know..."

"Good. Bring the bowl of Bollox bollocks."

Shayra handed him a carved wooden bowl of thick soup, a single plume of steam curled above it. Taking the bowl in his palms, Claudio raised it to his lips and gulped down the contents, a little embarrassed to realize how hungry he was. Apparently though he'd done the right thing – the squinting circle of villagers erupted into smiles and enthusiastic chirping. Then a larger bowl was passed in the circle, each member taking a swallow.

ß

Hand drums were pulled out and the priestess beat four times on her jangling corset to establish a rhythm. Like a living tambourine she pulsed her hips, the rhythm was at once earthy and ethereal. The sky reverently darkened, heavy black clouds blanketed the moon, and the torch fires throbbed to the beat. Then she swirled seductively, spinning low to glide her open palms over the surface of the land, and upward branching like a tree. Claudio somehow knew she'd become the forest spirit Deia. The old woman sang:

"Before the forest blanketed the world
All water, sky and land a swamp enswirled
And swimming through the darkness two forms bumped
Broad Deia and great Deio met and groped and thrashed and humped."

Claudio found himself drawn into the dance, and listening carefully he assumed the role of Deio.

"To breathe his scent she raised a tent of sky
To taste her breath he swept the seas aside
Then she became a leaf upon a breeze
And he a seed, she wrapped him up and thus they spawned the trees."

Just as he became a plant, she had become an animal. Her limbs and face flickered luminescent in the torchlight.

"She took the form of snuffalo enlarged
And he a heavy snuffalo, and charged
Then she a skrote, he pounced in matching form
In changing shapes they played and creatures of all kind were born.

Five billion years they played, then from up high
A flower-bulb in flame crash down from sky
A girl emerged, bright, curious and new
Along with her a creature, pungent, furious and blue."

In a flash Claudio glimpsed this circle from above, the forest glade ringed in torches, Bayla's dance, the horned man he realized was some version of himself. And in that moment he was the cloud, she was the forest and he ached, heavily, to pour himself over her. Now Shayra and Raydo entered the dance, becoming the girl and the Bollox.

"*She gathered pleasant fruits and smoked the herbs*

The monster slew some unicorns and birds
They cleared some forest, filled the land with seed
And multiplied and grew in greed and killed competing breeds."

Zayger burst into the circle, eyes wide, pointing in the distance, "The forest is burning, it's coming this way!"

All eyes turned to the dark forest – from between the trees they could see the light flashing in the distance.

Shaking off the trance, Claudio shouted "Maybe we can contain it!"

"No," Bayla took hold of his wrist. "We finish the dance."

A figure appeared, back-lit against the flame, running toward them. It was Donna, who dove on her knees to the circle and cried out, "Fire! Falco! The unkillable Captain is-- Dead!?" She wabbled and collapsed in a faint.

Raydo turned to Bayla, "Well *that's* good news at least but we've got to *do something* about the--"

"The *Thirteenth Moon is here* and we will *finish the dance.*" Bayla commanded. "The forest is in the care of the Gods."

"The Gods need *our* help. Shayra, you had a vision of fire. *You* tell us what to do."

All eyes turned to the apprentice. She looked at Bayla, then at Raydo. "And you'll do it?"

"Yes."

She closed her eyes, sighed and swiveled low, then high. The dance would resume.

"Great Deio sent the skowls to scorch the lands
The people starved, but Deia taught a dance
The Bollox limped away with shouldered blame
And Deio longed for Deia, and he kissed her with
the rain."

Claudio and Bayla met in the center and embraced. The torch-fires waved and lashed wildly in a swirling wind, then blinked out in unison as the air grew dense with mist.

"So that was the dance..." he said, as droplets of rain patted his head and shoulders approvingly.

"No," she smiled, with raindrops rolling down her cheeks, "*This* is the dance." Her fingers, strong but nimble, unfastened and peeled his pads and uniform as raindrops skittered down his body like electrical currents. Naked in near darkness he heard the low jangle and soft thuds of her clothing fall to the ground. Then she was pressed against him, radiating heat that pulsed through his veins. She pulled him down. The rainfall pressed and stroked, running over his shoulders like curious fingertips. Then it emboldened, heaving in waves that rocked the land, quickened to a storm lashing and pounding the forest. A flash of lightning and the surrounding villagers erupted in a thunderous applause.

Ring Seal, Crete, c1500BCE

SIXTH MOON

Six times the sea-green moon of Deia had emerged, a slim bashful curl glowing in the night sky.

Six times it matured and muscled, filling like a bowl to the brim.

Six times it plumped and rounded, till it shone pregnant and powerful in full turquoise blush.

Then six times it slimmed and withered, winnowing down to a crone's curved spine.

Six times it died, the night sky mourned in heavy black.

And then that shy young curl emerged again.

In other words, six months had gone by.

♭

The priestess and apprentice stepped into the glade, each carrying two squat wooden stools. The bangles and bracelets hanging from their corsets, wrists and ankles rung like wind-chimes. Bayla the high priestess had larger bangles that rung in dusky, seductive tones distinct from the bright tinkles of Shayra's slimmer beads. Combined they harmonized a song of power emerging and maturing.

Donna drifted silently behind them with four wooden basins. The Syndicate lieutenant still retained the loose jacket of her grey uniform to cover her brown breasts, otherwise exposed in the common leather bodice and short skirt of a Deian gardener. At some point the village children had dreadlocked her black hair, but she'd stopped them from painting blue spirals on her skin. Donna's head was tilted, eyes vacant, mouth hung slightly open. Her empty gaze softly alighted on a bold cluster of hungberry shrubs. Falco had tossed those seeds, and for six moons they'd grown, a final monument to the dead Captain. The bushes curled back their leaves and jutted their obscene pink berry-sacks.

Maybe Falco would have been proud.

Donna's curved black eyebrow twitched imperceptibly as the priestess and apprentice approached the bushes and pulled their blades. With gentle incisions they opened the sacks and fingered out two large berries from each, plopping them into the basins. They set these before the stools, sat and started squishing with their feet.

Bayla nodded and Donna blankly sank to a stool. She watched her feet step into a bowl and begin rhytmically churning.

ß

"They should be back by now," Bayla said, green eyes gazing off in the direction of the stream.

"And when are *you* gonna get back?" Shayra asked.

"...What?"

"Your feet are in those berries but your mind is off in the trees, with the hunters. With Kayno. You've been like this three days."

The priestess furrowed a heavy brow at her apprentice, then at the unoccupied fourth stool. "I meant *Grayda* should be here by now."

"And when did *she* become '*they*'?"

"Well she... She's much bigger now. And more diverse in temperament. Since she...*became 'they'* by getting pregnant, of course."

"And more belligerent than ever. She called Ayma an old prune-sack. And *you* a...paisley-plumed bostrich."

The priestess curled her broad shoulders back and pulled her elbows in like wings, jutting her massive breasts forward. Then she shook her heavy orange mane as her husky, muscular laughter jangled the beads of her corset and rang through the trees. "I know. That's why I invited her to crush hungberries with us. Nothing more calming than a good stomp-and-squish. Where is she?"

"Way up in that tall oak over there."

Bayla squinted as the sun touched her green eyes. "That oak?"

"No, the taller one. See that angry dot? She refuses to come down until Ayma changes her mind."

"Then I hope she brought blankets. Three moons of frost ahead."

"You'll be Ayma soon." The apprentice lowered her gaze, then cautiously raised it. "Would you have done the same?"

"Ayma's vision is dimming but she can still see that a pregnant girl needs a man ready to be a partner. Not just some boy she did the humpty-dance with in the woods."

"But don't we teach that the seed-planter shares in the harvest?"

"No." Bayla's glance sharpened under her heavy brow. "We teach that the one who *nurtures* the seed...will do what's best for the *tribe*. Gamer isn't ready yet. He still lives in his mother's tent, rolling bone-dice when he could be training for the hunter's trial. He's fourteen, there's only a year left for him to rise as a hunter or leave the tribe, anyway. If Grayda is so devoted to him, they can go to the desert together and she can find out whether he's a man or not."

Shayra dropped her small chin in respectful silence a moment, letting wild black curls fall over her bright brown eyes. Her wide nostrils flared.

Bayla waited, then said "Speak."

"You've always taught me that law should never be a line in the sand, but a wave on the shore, subject to time and lunar sway... You're changing." Shayra finally raised her eyes to meet Bayla's.

"*Yes* I'm changing. We're all changing. Creatures are changing into dirt, dirt is changing into plants, plants change into fruit, fruit changes into creatures, creatures are changing into dirt. Ayma is changing into moss. I'm changing into Ayma. You're changing into Bayla. Then one of our young girls will change into Shayra. We change and so does our feel of the law, that's why three together make decisions."

Shayra angrily slouched and glared sideways, "*You* think I'm not changing fast enough. Because you *want* to be Ayma. Puffing on that pipe all day and grooving to the voices of the forest."

Silence. A frisky breeze danced a purple leaf into the clearing, then awkwardly dropped it.

Bayla sighed. "When I was Shayra...*not* so long ago...I didn't feel ready, and nothing anybody said would have convinced me otherwise. There was only one person who could prove it to me, and now there's only one person who can prove it to *you*. Make the decision."

"About Grayda?"

"Yes. I'll be Ayma, you be Bayla and...I guess she can be Shayra for a moment." Bayla nodded toward Donna, who continued blankly squishing. "You've heard Ayma's answer. What should Bayla say?"

ƺ

Shayra lifted her chin and closed her eyes. The sunlight was wild pink on her closed lids but gradually calmed to a rich crimson. She breathed in deep through her wide nostrils, then exhaled. "Ayma hears the spirits that a baby needs a father, not just a seed-injector. And she's right that Nayzo is a keen tracker, and maybe someday won't wake the whole village with his snoring. He's ready for partnerhood. But if Grayda chooses Gamer, then *he* should be given a choice. Succeed in the trials and become a hunter before the baby comes to light, be a father, or take his dice to the desert. If Grayda must be angry, she should be angry at Gamer."

Bayla lifted her palms. "Here we are."

"Really?"

"Bayla's decision is made."

"*...Really?*"

"You can let them know once we're finished here. These berries won't squish themselves. Donna. Those look just right."

The lieutenant froze and slowly retracted her feet. Bayla pulled the basin and placed the fourth one in front of her. Donna resumed joylessly mashing.

ß

"They should be back by now," Bayla said again, gazing off in the direction of the stream.

"Will you stop looking over there? Deia will return the hunters with food or she'll feed them to the forest. Life continues either way."

"I know."

"You *know*, but your mind is mashed as that berry sauce. You're in love."

Bayla shot the apprentice a quizzical glance. Then she calmed and shrugged, "Of course. The priestess loves Kayno, so it's always been."

"But you didn't look off into the woods like that when you were married to Grazer."

"Grazer I had known all my life, the great hunter, warrior, dancer. Becoming Kayno, Grazer always knew what to do. When it came time to make Kayno's drum, Grazer split the gourd, pulled the skin and beat down firm and steady. Claudio's first two tries were a mess."

Shayra smiled into the distance. "The children cried. That poor gourd."

"It's all so new to him but he *feels* it, he learns, and with a little guidance... Now he grips the drum and his fingers send subtle messages – a strong and confident rhythm...with flourishes, nuances, a depth of feeling..."

"...Are we still talking about the drum? Or are we talking about the humpty-dance now?"

Bayla blushed and looked away. "Crush your berries."

"We don't even *need* sauce. *You* just want your toes to taste like berries when he gets back."

"Maybe," Bayla smirked, raising an eyebrow. "Maybe I'm going to *wear* the sauce when he gets back."

ß

Zayger the huntress dashed into the glade and landed in a dramatic stance, teeth flashing, dreadlocks streaming and sinewy limbs extended. "The hunters return," she rasped in her deepest voice, "so *heavy* with success we can barely drag our sacks. Aaaaaaaand?"

Raydo and Claudio walked in, laughing, the young hunter rubbing his arm against the ensign-turned-chieftain's shoulder. "Zayger bags the most game," Claudio nodded, shoving him away.

"As always," Raydo rubbed against Claudio again and giggled.

Donna looked up dully, gazed from chin to chin, then hung her head and continued mashing berries. Zayger did a little victory jig. "ZAYGER!" She sat down like a bear and began eating fistfulls of mashed berry from a bowl.

Shayra leapt to her feet, sloshing some berry-juice from the basin. She launched herself in an embrace for Raydo but he side-stepped and she landed behind him, confused.

With a steady gaze on Claudio, Bayla calmly wiped her feet and stepped languidly to him. "Where are the others?"

"By the stream, washing and skinning."

"All bones and stones intact thanks to

Kayno," Zayger said, some berry ooze dripping down her chin. "One of us *did* get sprayed by a circle of scutter-punks."

Shayra giggled at Raydo. "Is *that* what that smell is?"

"They would have punked me to death, but he yawned and they scattered." Once again Raydo leaned in to rub his shoulder against Claudio.

Claudio pushed him. "It was nothing compared to the time you pried me out from under a pregnant Smellophant."

"And Kayno showed us, instead of waiting for Skrotes to steal gungan eggs, we could just rob the nest ourselves, then sneak up on skrotes while they were humping mushrooms."

Zayger, mouth full, sputtered berry juice while gesturing widely, "We've got skrotes and eggs like never before!"

Shayra looked at Raydo, "I hope you left enough to hatch the next generation."

"Yes, he counted the females," he said, then turned to Claudio, nodding in reverence at his antlers, then looking into his brown eyes. "I doubted you. But you're nothing like that swaggering, overbearing tin-plated dic--"

Shayra put a finger to his lips. "*Raydo.* Don't speak ill of the dead."

"Sorry. I'm proud to hunt with you. Kayno."

"You honor me," Claudio said, "with your assistance, your advice. I'd be a mockery of Kayno, without you. And the village knows it, and they're grateful." The young hunter nodded respectfully and extended his arms for an embrace. "But *seriously* back off, go rinse in the stream." They laughed.

Shayra snatched up a basin and stepped toward Raydo. "Here. Scrub with this."

"What, and smell like a wife who doesn't get licked enough?"

"I've had a vision of your future – it's *berry* sweet." She pulled the basin back to dump it on him.

"No!" Raydo sprinted into the woods.

"Don't be afraid, I've got *berry* good news for you." Shayra chased him, cheery giggles mixing with the bright jingle of her anklets and beads.

"Zayger," Claudio said, "head to the stream. Those skrotes aren't gonna shave themselves."

"I'll be...*berry*...back soon..? … Swish-boom-Zayger." She said, and leapt out of the clearing.

ƺ

Claudio stepped up to Bayla and breathed her scent. He slid a hand around the small of her back and pulled her close. Then she surrounded him with her long brawny limbs and wide frame, he felt a familiar pop in his lower back that momentarily melted his knees to jelly. Bayla's embraces had frightened him a bit at first, especially when he was returning from a long hunt. But after six moons he couldn't remember a time he'd imagined loving someone smaller than he was. He tilted his chin back and kissed her. His toes lost touch with the ground.

She set him down and gently shoved his shoulders back, carefully eyeing him from head to foot and up again. He was not wounded.

Claudio caught his breath and whispered, "Here we are."

"Here we are. Come with me." She wrapped

his hand in hers.

"*Yes,*" he grinned, then sighed. "Soon as we've finished skinning and cooking--"

"*Or*, how about right *now?*"

"I-- Kayno can't be resting while the others are--"

She raised an eyebrow. "They'll know you're not resting. Kayno has important responsibilities to the priestess." She winked. "'And the village knows it, and they're grateful.'"

ᛉ

Claudio pulled his hand away and squinted at her a moment. "This is a test. ...Is this a test?"

"What's a... 'test'?"

"You, with the fruit under these trees? Are you trying to tempt me?"

She jutted a hip and clapped a hand to it. "I didn't think I'd have to *try.*"

"There was an old story..." Claudio tried to remember it.

"In *our* sacred story the naked woman under the tree made the man *very*, very happy and it went on and on for*ever...* Or until two minutes ago, apparently."

"There's nowhere I'd rather be than where you are, naked, but I..."

She turned to show him her profile and raised her chin. "...So? If you're in such a hurry to stand in a cold stream flaying dead animals, why aren't you down there now?"

"I just had to see you. Even after half a year, sometimes off on the hunt I think it must have been some dream, you and me, our hump-tent, the wonder in your eyes when you look at the stars. Seeing you laugh in the purple rain. Waking up just in time watch you dress... I'm afraid I'll wake up again, on that cold starship, waiting for my turn to horribly die on another one of Falco's exotic missions."

"Nope. Right now an exotic mission is beckoning *you* into a warm tent, and you're rushing off to stand in cold water with naked men."

♭

Bayla surveyed Claudio's face and body. It had taken weeks for him to give up his ill-fitting uniform, piece by piece, but now he looked so natural in his hunter gear. The leather pads and straps accentuated his broad shoulders and narrow waist. And the blue peaks on his face and arms were luminescent against his bronzed skin. The paint seemed to hover just above the surface. The headband had mostly disappeared into his shiny black curls, and through selfless acts he'd earned additional points for his antlers.

But she'd waited long enough and turned to go.

"How are preparations for winter?" he asked.

She stopped. "About half of the crops are buried for storage, we should be set before the frost hits tonight. Then we dig up the wine-jars we planted in summer."

"Did the Skrayter and Bayner clans settle their dispute over that big gourd?"

"They fought all day, then drank together all

night, a baby or two on the way, all one happy clan now."

"And what about Grayda? Did she agree to marry Nayzo?"

"We've decided it should be Gamer's choice, grow up or go away."

"Good. Nayzo's ready to be a father, but he's afraid Grayda would tell the whole village he snores. I'll talk with Gamer tonight and get him started on the hunter trial preparations."

"He looks up to you."

"And I'm tired of looking up into that tree. It's a good resolution."

"It was Shayra. She's ready, I see it in her, blossoming with every day. I've known two Baylas and do my best to maintain, but what she'll be capable of I've never--" Bayla's green eyes had brightened but suddenly she gasped. A heavy gloom had sunk the slabs of Claudio's features. Staring into the blue moss he took a slow deep breath. He looked smaller. She laid a hand on his shoulder, which made him appear smaller still, and his eyes flicked over to Donna.

"What about Donna? Any change?"

Bayla had forgotten Donna was still there, blankly churning. "Still not a word. Her tent is tidy, her garden patch is neat, she mashes berries and tans hides faster than I do. She doesn't even seem unhappy, but she's..."

"Shut down."

"If she got pregnant, Ayma could choose her a partner. But she hasn't responded to any of the hunters and we've seen some *really* impressive feather-dances."

"Six full moons since Falco died in that fire and still not one word."

"I know you have...urgent barbecue business to attend, but before you go to the stream would you take a moment, at least *try* talking to her?"

"Yes. There's something in the tent I think she might respond to." His distant gaze returned to her green eyes. One of his cheeks bunched in a half-grin. "Maybe we could go get it...together..?"

The priestess smiled. "No, you were right. Kayno. I'll go share news that soon we *all* get our hunters back. See you at the party." And she walked away, weaving some extra sway into her steps. He stared after her broad hips and wide, powerful thighs till she was out of sight. Then he listened till the low, seductive chiming of her bracelets and beads faded into the sounds of the forest.

ß

"Donna. I know you can hear me," Claudio leaned in and stared hard. Her dark eyes didn't move. "Lieutenant," he put a hand on her shoulder. No response. "*Lieutenant.*"

He shook his head and lumbered out of the clearing toward the village.

Silence, and the rhythmic sloshing of berry sauce.

A curious little jackanape skittered down from a tree and poked its head into the glade. It looked like a combination rabbit monkey with tall ears and a shiny red bottom. Sniffing around and sensing no danger it hopped up to the basin and cocked its head at Donna.

"Yip-yap. Yup," it barked. This was jackanese for "Food me. Dead-or-alive."

She didn't respond. Hooking its front paws to the rim, the jackanape darted its muzzle into the bowl and sucked up a cheekful of warm sauce. Then it raised its face and watched Donna while gulping it down.

"You can put your ray-gun to *my* head, space-babe," Donna heard the Captain's voice behind her.

Her body snapped upright at full attention, abs tight, chest out, feet still in the bowl. "Captain." The jackanape yeeped and skittered off into the brush.

"You make me wish I had three hands...and two flippers," his voice again, getting closer. "And some tentacles too." A crackle of twigs.

"Where are you?" Donna turned around to face the sound. She saw Claudio in his Deian clothing and paint, holding the Captain Falco action figure. Mint condition, uniform perfect, shiny plastic hair.

"We *never* surrender..." it said, *"Except...to the rhythm."*

ꭗ

"Give me that." Donna darted a long, limber arm for the action figure.

"No," Claudio side-stepped.

"You stole it."

"One of the hunters found it in the search. Falco must have dropped it while flailing off into the forest-fire."

"And you've hidden it all this time."

"Yes. I mean I don't...whatever, *play* with it."

"Does *she* know about it? That space-vixen? You've kept it in *her* tent."

"*Nobody* plays with it."

"You mock him, you two mock the talking Captain and he can't even stand up for himself!"

"It would balance better without this big head."

"Give it to me, it's not yours. It's not fair." She snatched for it again.

"What, are you five years old?"

"Says the kid who won't *share the toy!*"

"*Stand back.*"

Donna's brown skin visibly paled, her eyes widened, "Don't hurt him!"

"It's *not* the Captain!"

"It's all we have left!"

"We have our *lives* left – *you* should be living yours. We're in this magical forest with honest people who want to share joys and sorrows--"

"But they'll *never* understand us like *he* could."

Claudio couldn't contain a laugh. "What? He thought *you* were an action figure."

"*Who's* the action figure? *You're* a boy-toy in the hands of that abundantly cliche'd alien enchantress. She colors her hair – that's not natural. With the blood of scratterpillars, rolls them up like toothpaste tubes, I've seen her do it while you're out hunting. Smells like grogg-vomit. How enchanting is *that?*"

Claudio was perplexed. In half a year Donna had been like a ghost – he'd wondered if in a delayed reaction to a concussion she might have lost the ability to speak. But here she was talking rapidly and gesturing aggressively. The sound of a twig snap alerted him that he'd been backed to the edge of the clearing.

He squared his broad shoulders but remained calm. "Everybody knows she colors her hair, she's not allowed to go gray until she becomes Ayma. And what does that have to do with-- Stay back."

ƅ

Donna fixated on the action figure in Claudio's hand. "So why now? Why wait half a year?"

"I didn't think it would *take* half a year. You're one of the best navigators in the Syndicate, a decorated lieutenant--"

"And *you're* a security officer, you had *one* responsibility," she pecked his chest with her finger so hard he almost fell backward. "To get killed protecting the Captain. Instead you let him die on this Santa-forsaken planet and stashed away his irresistible toy for your fanboy collection – *give him to me.*"

"No. You need to let him go."

"*You're* the one who memorized his exhilarating stories, his delicious catch-phrases and thrilling maneuvers. *You're* his biggest fan."

"I was never more than vice secretary in the Falco-pals club."

"And now with him out of the way, *you're* acting out a Starbuck magazine alien sex-fantasy."

"That is not-- Stand back."

She leaned in close and scanned his face with her eyes, scalp to chin and up again. Donna stared right through the antlers and glossy black curls, through the triangles of blue facepaint to the noble golden skin, the rocky features, the heroic brown eyes. They were the eyes of a leader. "Somehow I didn't see it."

"I'll break the toy." His voice quivered.

"The toy is not Falco. *You* are."

"*Hey*. Back off."

Donna clamped his shoulders in her hands.

"Let me go..." He winced, she was stronger than he'd thought. "I'm not the Captain..."

Her smooth brown face approached his and tilted. "Captain..."

ᛉ

"*Who's* the Captain?" Falco's voice. Triumphantly he stepped into the glade.

"Captain!" Donna released Claudio, whose backside thudded to the ground.

He sat up and rubbed his lower back. "*Captain..?*"

There he was. In mint condition. Uniform impeccable, not one hair out of place. The heroic jaw, the defiant sideburns, the sky-blue eyes, the dancer's physique. A slight breeze whistled the surrounding reeds in a taut brassy crescendo, billowed his kilt like a flag and lifted a leafy branch so a ray of sunlight could glint his perfect white teeth. "What's with the surprise? You knew I'd be back."

Claudio shook his head and stood. "It's true. Vanishing in flame never kills anyone important."

Donna darted to him, "But it can leave a scar – are you scarred?"

"Of *course* not."

"A thorough physical exam is--"

"I assumed you were both familiar with my academy Scotch-winning master's thesis. 'The Captain Stages His Death.' Later published by the title... 'Back That Asteroid and Batter Up.'"

Donna's hand shot up, "I read both versions."

"In Captain's Log magazine...I don't recall the issue number..?" Falco raised a brow at Claudio.

"...Six forty-two..." Claudio mumbled.

"Good to know you're still sharp, ensign. And lieutenant, of course you remember when we were trapped aboard the Milli-Vanillium Falcon."

"You hid under a pile of dead security officers, yes, and then disguised yourself as a fly-girl dance instructor!"

"Also the time I poisoned myself into a death-like state for the second act of *Our Town on Ice*."

ß

"But where have you been?" Claudio demanded, "You ran off into the woods, talking to a seed-bar..."

Falco smirked. "The seed-bar and I *did* have a rather interesting negotiation. And it was *right*. The soil here is *perfect* for barley, but all these shady *trees* want it for themselves."

Donna urgently touched his shoulder. "I remember – you were scared of the trees."

"I...needed them to *think* I was scared," Falco pirouetted out of her reach. "Lull them into a false sense of security, trees are stupid that way. Look at them. Always lurking in the background, patiently executing their conspiracy, sinister...photo-*synthesis?* No one ever told us what it *was*..."

"Plants make oxygen." Claudio rolled his eyes.

"Plants make *slaves*. You can't see it because your mind is imprisoned in the bio-matrix. Trees only give us oxygen so *we* can supply *them* with precious carbon dioxide."

"But really, it's a fair trade. Billions of years, no one's complained."

"Wake up and smell the chlorophyll! The trees are listening. You know what they call people like you? A *sap*."

Donna sputtered stiff giggles. "'A sap'!" Her high-pitched tittering lowered into hee-haws as she doubled over and slapped her thigh. Falco and Claudio glanced at each other and shook their heads. Donna's deep guffaws lightened to girlish giggles again as she clapped Falco on the shoulder, then began rubbing his chest.

The Captain shoved her hand away. "*Lieutenant! Pull* yourself together. It *wasn't* that *funny*."

Claudio grumbled, "*I* don't think she thought it was funny at *all*."

"Well who made *you* the king of comedy? Besides your stylist? Seriously. Ensign. Someone has painted on your face. Also you have antlers now. And also..." Falco gestured Claudio's leather shoulder-pads and briefs, "Also all *this*. Whatever it is, and whatever it makes these hippie wastoids think of you. The 2160's are *over*."

"The trees are part of this community, we cooperate--"

"A spoonful of oxygen and you'll believe *anything*."

"Those flower-spores, they messed with your mind."

"I say again. *'Antlers.' You've* been living an adolescent space-fantasy with a kinky alien sorceress. *She's* been catatonic for six months. We *all* inhaled the spores, *I* did something *constructive* while *you* geeked out."

Donna stood at attention. "It told you to attack the trees... You started that forest fire."

"And it *worked*. One acre of forest ash, one crumbled seed-bar, the yield is incredible. I always *knew* it was my destiny, spreading seed across the galaxy, I just didn't understand *how* until *now*."

♭

"But..." Claudio was momentarily confused to hear a phrase formulating in his mind, "Slash-and-burn farming? No, I can't let you. Calvin..."

Falco's muscles tensed and his warm green eyes frosted over in cold blue. His body contracted. "Don't. You. *Ever* call me that!"

Claudio winced at the crackle of anger and betrayal in Falco's voice. Also at Falco's blurry fist which dug into his abdomen. The Captain was in battle-mode. Claudio got lucky with two flails, sweeping aside punches at his jaw and gut, but his third flail was apparently predictable, and a series of impacts – chin, gut, forehead, chest, nose, chest again – battered his body like a meteor shower. Falco swept gracefully back, like a painter eyeing an unfinished masterpiece. Claudio wanted to fall but his rubbery knees couldn't take the message, and his eyes refused to miss a single cinematic moment of Falco in action. The Captain's body, a dream-ballet of a billion-dollar golf-swing, channeled its full force into a single knuckle that hooked Claudio's chin, raising him from the ground. He floated a moment in the air. Then the floor of the glade clobbered every part of his back at once.

Falco hadn't missed a breath. His hand swooped down like a hawk, taking hold of the action figure, held it close to Claudio's ear and pressed the button.

"You may *call* me...*Captain*," it said.

ß

Donna, who'd been swaying with melodramatic gestures of suspense during the fight, waited for Falco to rise and then swooned into his arms. *"Captain..."* she said breathlessly.

"Wow, you're...heavier than I remember," Falco said, dumping her to the ground.

She clambered up quickly. "But why wait so long to let us know? We could have helped."

"You *were* helping. By infiltrating this...alien love-nest, learning their savage lifestyle. I'm sure our deep and lengthy debrief will be most gratifying."

This combination of words caused her to lose control of her bottom jaw, it hung slack, but she managed to force out the syllables "I *will*-- It. It *will*."

"And when this nerd gets his head out of the

role-playing game..."

Claudio rolled onto his belly and tried to lift himself, grunting "I'll *never* join you."

"Quote scripture all you want but you've *already* joined. You took an oath to the Syndicate. Break it and face exile on the de*serter* planet. Which, for some reason, is covered in gumdrops and cupcakes... But I've heard it all tastes like *licorice.*"

Donna sneered, "The licorice taste of *betrayal*, a black web--"

"I think he gets it, lieutenant."

Claudio stood, clutching his rib, "But the Deians...they haven't done any wrong."

"They've ensnared your mind, fed you nothing but lies...and testicles... Trapped you in their crazy pagan game. But don't you see? *They're* trapped in it too. I don't want to *hurt* these creatures – I want to *help* them."

"Here we go..."

"They're so busy getting huggy with the trees they can't see what the forest is hiding - a goldmine of rich topsoil."

Donna raised a finger. *"Brown gold.* Of *course..."*

"I'll negotiate with Brazil, full developing-planet package. A school here, a hospital there, Animatronic Santa's Village and eighteen coffee shops."

"Nineteen." Donna said, "So the *other* eighteen can be where all the *losers* hang out." She slithered an arm around Falco's waist but he obliviously pivoted away.

Claudio stood taller, though it racked his torso in coursing sensations of pain. *"Come on* Captain, *you know* full well that 'development' is only Syndicate-speak for appropriating property, pushing politics, poverty and pollution. It's a completely parasitic--"

"I gather *today's* histrionic monologue is brought to us by the letter 'P.'"

Donna slapped her knee, then sidled up to shake hands with Falco. "Swish, boom," they said.

"These people don't need the Syndicate, they've got traditions--"

"I've seen their traditions. One day I watched all the tribal women bounding naked through the woods, intoxicated, tearing live animals to pieces with their teeth. It was the most terrifying and...titillating thing I've ever witnessed. If they'd seen me they would have--"

"Torn you to pieces too, yes, that's why the hunters and children hide during the Sparagmophagia."

"Well there's going to be *new* traditions. Intoxicated, naked? Fine, but the rest is *over*. I haven't been so sickened since the Venus Vegas floor-show that...doubled as an all-you-can-eat buffet."

In a flash of sinewy limbs and viney dreadlocks, Zayger leapt into the glade and landed sitting crosslegged at the Captain's feet. "Are you telling the story about the all-you-can-eat Vegas kick-line? Start from when you won your ticket by pit-wrestling the Abominatrix."

"Zayger?" Claudio squinted, "...*You* know

that story?"

The huntress rocked back and forward in satisfaction. "Zayger knows *all.* The stories."

Falco nodded for her to rise. "We're not doing Falco-piece theater right now. Status report."

"The blue harvest is almost in, the meats are smoking for tomorrow, first frost. And Zayger grabbed the most skrotes!"

"Well done, private."

They did the Syndicate handshake. "Swish, boom."

ß

From the clearing's edge, Raydo had watched Zayger do the shake, swish and boom with the Captain. The sight of his friend beaming with adoration brought the young hunter bounding in rage, the blue triangles on his cheeks glowing against the heat of his anger. "*You!*"

Falco turned to him and smiled. "Are you ready to dance, Tigerlilly?"

Raydo threw himself at Falco but found his body restrained in a knot of arms. He swung his head back to see Claudio clutching him in place.

"So you *do* still remember your job," Donna cocked an eyebrow and put a hand on her hip.

"My job is the safety of the hunters. Breathe, Raydo, he's still Captain Falco..."

Raydo yanked himself free and turned to face Claudio. "Of course. I remember now. 'Ensign swears to protect the captain and Syndicate property by his gruesome death.' The Captain's back and *you're protecting* him."

Zayger hopped in protest, "Captain Falco *never* uses protection. And with hands like that he doesn't *need* a reach-around from some heavy *petty officer.*"

Falco stepped forward "Zayger."

"He could spank off every man in this tribe."

Donna flashed a look, "What are you *teaching* this kid?"

Raydo glared at Zayger, "You've been helping him too..."

"He helps him*self.* With his bare hands. But yeah, sometimes I grab his skrote for him."

Falco barked "*Zayger.* That's enough."

"We went through the *trials* together. We were children, I was the first person to call you Zayger. And in all our lives you've never been able to keep a secret. How could you have kept this from me? For half a year..."

"Falco said if I told you, your face would get puffy and you'd whine out 'why are you doing this?'"

"But *why* are--" Raydo caught himself and gasped. His eyes darted rage at Falco and confusion at Zayger. "What am I supposed to say *now?*"

ʒ

Falco assumed one of his statue poses and surveyed the tips of his fingernails. Perfect. "The intelligent question would be '*How* are you doing this?' But your primitive jungle mind couldn't understand. So all *you* need to know is *that* we're doing this, it's for your own good, and there's no stopping it."

A low powerful voice quaked his stomach.

"And just what do 'we' intend to do?" With a tolling of musical beads, the priestess strode into the glade, followed by her lightly chiming apprentice, "Calvin."

Falco swiveled sharply on his heel to face her. His look was cool till the sight of her bounteous and powerful body stretched his eyes involuntarily wide and he struggled to regain his gaze of indifference. "Bayla, priestess of Deia. So voluptuous and yet so...*oblivious.*"

"That you've been hiding out in the forest, planting grain in the ashes of the fire you set."

Shayra spun her head to look at Bayla's eyes, alarmed by her calm, "Planting *grain?* But Bayla, that means--"

"I know what it means."

"But you didn't tell me! Our crops, everything could be destroyed! Raydo, warn the hunters, I'll tell the harvesters."

Raydo sprinted toward the stream and Shayra turned to run for the village. Bayla laid a hand on her shoulder. "Shayra. Ask Ayma how much time we have." The apprentice sprinted from the clearing and Bayla turned her broad jaw and large green eyes to Falco. "You're not curious what comes next?"

"Savages scampering around, I presume."

Zayger cautiously approached, her head cocked to the side "...What's gonna happen?"

"Something that hasn't happened in hundreds of years. The skowls will follow the chaff of the grain on the wind."

"But that's just an old story, to scare us. Nobody's every seen one."

"You'll see them soon."

♭

Like a celebrity on tour, Falco visited each pair of wide eyes with a reassuring flash of cold blue gaze, marble features and granite jaw. Claudio faced him with anger, Donna with adoration and Zayger with gaping hope. He turned back to Bayla. "You don't scare me. If you've known what I've been doing, you've accidentally revealed there's no danger. How *did* you know?"

"You're not very mysterious."

"Not if you're spying on me."

"Peeping is a man's game. You've watched the Wild Rumpus, the Celebration of the Lizard, spied on us bathing, occasionally crept over just to watch the tribe eat. You hide yourself well, from the eye. But I know the scent of every native-born Deian, every creature and tree. You, Calvin Falco, are quite distinctive – virility, motility, and a dash of nobility. I could find you blindfolded in a rainstorm."

The others cautiously inched in, to confirm this with a subtle sniff at Falco.

"The surprise is you *didn't*. Though you've been stalking me with your...foxy snout. But maybe you're just-- Everybody *stop that!* Back off."

"It's just...um," Donna said as they stepped away.

"Petition the toy company for a scratch-and-sniff action figure, but *everybody get out of my space.*" He locked eyes with the priestess again. "Except *you* – *you get in* my space *right now.*"

♭

Bayla smiled patiently, the slightest hint of joy colored her broad cheeks. With a delicate grace and a prize-fighter's swagger she stepped up and stood nose-to-nose with Falco. "Isn't it *all* your space, Calvin?"

"That's right. Call me that again. I know you love to."

"No."

"Because *you're* captain here, these childish hippies, all swept up in your abundant heaping charisma. And then one day you see my jaw-line, registered trademark, glinting teeth, bold and defiant sideburns... By which I mean you...*breathe* in deep my unmistakable musk, urgent with energy, pungent with...pugnacity..? You can't stand it."

"...Is that my cue? What's my line? Clearly you've been rehearsing this scene without me."

"You think I'm some stock character, a generic hero in a series of episodic adventures."

"Well...*aren't* you?"

"Not here, not this time. I knew it the day we arrived, you accidentally fell for the ensign, it was like the whole story-arc veered off into some...twisted alternate time-line."

"Some people get rejected, look at their reflection in water and say 'you're okay.' They don't need to invent a parallel reality."

"Yes, rejection is a new frontier for me. But don't you *see?*"

"...I have no idea what you're going to say."

"That's right. Because *this time* the Captain is *off book,*" Falco couldn't contain a dancer's flourish, which also strategically placed him a pace back from her looming muscular body. "Improvising. And it feels *great*."

"So this is the new unpredictable Calvin Falco. Who landed on an exotic planet, stripped her bare and sprayed his seed."

"Wait a--"

"What you've done to Deia – how is it different from your formulaic series of episodic conquests?"

"...*What?* Look. You're confused, I'm confused. You've mistaken a cameo for a star and I'm...maybe I *am* impregnating a planet. I'm sure there's a publishable story in it. But you and me, we can still fix this paradox before it potentially obliterates the galaxy. I've got a hammock--"

Claudio stepped up, *"Captain."*

"I *told* you never to call me-- Oh. You said 'Captain,' right?"

Bayla stared him down sternly. "Calvin," she said.

ß

Raydo and Shayra returned simultaneously, breathless, she handed Bayla a satchel. "Ayma said to give you this."

"I'll kill you..." Raydo glared.

"Raydo, no." Bayla said.

Falco kept his eyes on the priestess. "Lieutenant, in the pod there's another box of seed-bars, we'll need that. And some fuel and flares and a bottle of Scotch."

"But Captain..." Donna stared hard at Bayla.

"I'll be fine," he nodded and Donna ran

toward the pod. "Hey I know you guys have urgent...idiotic scurrying to do. Don't let *me* stop you."

A quaking rose through Raydo's body till it rattled his head. "I'LL KILL YOU!" And he charged at Falco, recklessly throwing every limb in quick succession, only to see them dodged in graceful flowing motions – the Captain was dancing. The hunter stopped a moment, puzzled and breathing hard. Claudio and Shayra reached to grasp his wrists but he evaded and charged once again with all he had, jabbing with his knuckles, knees, feet and forehead, touching nothing. Smiling serenely Falco swiveled and swayed, swooped and swerved as if the furious attack were a gentle melody.

Pausing again to catch his breath, Raydo peered at his fists, wondering a moment if his body had somehow ceased to be solid. Then he heard a slight crackle and saw Falco's boot, twisting into the ground, locking into place to launch him for a counter-attack. Falco's face, unblushed by the onslaught, his eyes cold blue, a tip of his lip curling into a grin.

Raydo's jaw dropped, his knees wobbled, his stomach sunk.

The Captain leapt.

ß

Claudio caught Falco in mid-air, heaving his padded shoulder into the Captain's ribs. Knocked aside, Falco landed on his toes and twisted to let Claudio's momentum crash him head-first into the moss. Shayra leapt, slashing and clawing she descended at him from above. He side-stepped, a paternal kick to the backside helping her along toward a roll on the ground.

"Stay down, Tinkerbell, I don't want to hurt you."

Then they all charged at once.

Claudio lurched low and Shayra launched herself high, Bayla threw her full force frontal and Zayger timidly punched from the back. Raydo lifted himself and found an opening in the fray of fists and feet, swipes and swings, to jab a blade at Falco's neck. And there at the center of this chaotic tornado of reckless assault, the Captain smiled and kept dancing. It was the work-out he'd been waiting for, six long months alone, and he wanted to enjoy every moment.

Sensing the patterns, he easily set his body into a routine of shimmies and twirls, then adjusted slightly so he could watch Bayla's face, blushed with determination, grunting and thrusting with the tidal force of her brawny body rolling into his space, rolling out. Yes, he mused wistfully, this was her sexual face. And she was quite a fighter too! She froze a second and recoiled, sensing she'd been watched, and pierced Falco with a look of admonition. His cheeks involuntarily bunched in a boyish grin. Then a sensation he'd never felt before – an angry fist had grazed his hair. The priestess's apprentice had touched his hair. Captain Calvin Theseus Falco's hair.

His lips tightened in a frosty glower. This had gone too far.

An elbow to Claudio's ear laid him out flat on the ground. A clutch on Raydo's knife-wielding wrist, a quick sharp twist, and the boy was on his knees. A swerve at his waist matched Zayger's two fists into the foreheads of the priestess and apprentice. As expected, the huntress pulled back in fright, a perfunctory bop on the head and she collapsed like a severed marionette.

Then like a carpenter fixing floor-boards he went around administering a quick thigh-punch to the ones who were trying to get back up. Approaching Bayla last he went a bit pale – the annoyance of this brawl was nothing compared to the flurry of protocols and personal directives that would be breached in touching this magnificent priestess. Seeing his demeanor turn grimly bashful, she spared him by sitting in dignified stillness. He discretely bobbed his jaw in gratitude.

♭

Falco cautiously ran three fingers through his hair. Still perfect. He breathed in relief and then smiled at the five figures wincing and clutching themselves on the forest floor. Clapping his hands to rouse them he enthusiastically called out, "Everybody rest up a moment, then round up some more hunters and charge again. This time I'm going to fight...*left*-handed. With a *Latin* flair."

"No," Claudio groaned. "Ow... How did you...*do* that?"

"You of all people should know. I *am Captain. Calvin. Theseus. Falco*. I do my own hair *and* my own stunts."

Raydo clutched his wrist, cautiously uncurling his fingers. "I... I thought..."

"That I was swaggering, overbearing and tin-plated? That my talk was bigger than my walk? Very much the opposite. A Syndicate Captain *always* speaks with humility. I've been thrown into countless coliseums, arenas and jello-pits all over the galaxy."

Zayger smiled meekly, "You should hear his story about...defeating that hairy roller-derby squad...the Wendigo Girls..."

"*And* I once brawled the cast of Disney's *Scarlet-Letter-the-Musical,* rescued Hester Prynne, now she wears an 'F,' for--" *Zzitt,* a sizzling sound, Falco looked down to see a small hole burning into his boot. "HEY! That *bird* just...crapped acid on my boot. And I think he did it on *purpose.*"

Everyone else looked up, terrified. First a single black bird, angular and sharp, then three more and then hundreds streaked the sky like black vapor-trails.

Bayla scanned the frightened faces and nodded. "The skowls are here."

♭

Zzitt, a droplet burned through a leaf and seared into Raydo's shoulder. He grunted, pathetically trying to stifle a yowl. *Zzitt, Zzitt, Zzitt,* Shayra clapped a hand to her cheek, seared by a drop and Claudio clutched his arm. Then the quickening rhythm of *Zzitt-Zzitt-Zzitt* became an electric buzzing, acid drips scorching holes in the moss, burning everyone as they writhed and yelped in agony. Everyone except Captain Falco who stood straight, staring angrily down at the hole in his boot.

He spat on it, then wiped it off on Claudio.

Raydo crawled over and arched his torso to shelter Shayra. "It's a cluster-flock!"

"Heh," Falco smirked, "What *else* is new on Deia? Wait, did you say 'flock'?"

"Bayla! Get down!" Claudio called, trying to cover her.

She shoved him aside, "Let me go." She pulled four turtle-shell rattles from the satchel and handed him two. "Do what I do." She began a dance, the turtle-shells rustling low and her beads ringing in harmony.

"Of course," he grunted, following along. "It *had* to be dancing." *Zzitt.* "Ow!"

ƀ

In the midst of the acid crap-storm, with cries of fear and pain rising from the nearby village and people crawling on the ground in pain, Falco was mesmerized by Bayla and Claudio dancing. Surely this, of all he'd witnessed on this world, was the most stupid thing he'd seen. And yet it was so consistent with what he'd observed that he almost felt he could comprehend it.

The priestess's body was hypnotic, vibrating with the rattle-shakes and rhythmic stomps, Falco inwardly winced to think of acid burns marking her exposed skin, he longed to break protocol and drag her into the pod for shelter but knew she'd fight him to the death to protect her right to do this idiotic dance. He snuffed in anger and let his mind open the floodgates of snide, dismissive comments for this. There were too many, his eyes widened, quips flickered through his brain so fast he couldn't choose one to say. But he couldn't just stand there with his mouth open either, so he clicked his heels together and decided to look distinguished.

Donna stepped into the glade, surveyed the scene of suffering, fixed her stare on the Captain and elected to mimic his composure despite the burning drops on her skin. She approached him, holding forth a broken glass bulb. "The Scotch bottle... It's dead, Captain."

Falco gently accepted the wreckage and balanced it on the fingertips of his outstretched hand, "Alas, poor Yonni-Walker... A fellow of most...excellent fancy..."

"It's *working!*" Claudio called out as fingers of sunshine poked through the black cloud, "they're afraid of the sound!"

Falco looked up, the sky was indeed clearing. Then he saw where the birds had turned to. "They're heading for my grain! Lieutenant! Follow me!" He sprinted off and Donna followed.

ß

Raydo lifted a fist toward the sky, "Curse you, Falco!" And a drop of acid plopped searing into his eye.

"Raydo!" Hearing the sizzle, seeing the smoke, Shayra twisted to cover him.

"Stay down!" he shouted, shoving her back beneath him.

The last drizzles fizzled to silence on the moss, now blackened in patches that looked and smelled of disease.

"Raydo, your eye..." Shayra reached for him as he stood.

"It's gone." Raydo said, covering the melted pit with his palm. He sniffed the air. "And our food is destroyed."

"I'll take you to Ayma."

"Get away from me!" he snapped his body away and swiveled toward Bayla. "Shayra had a vision of the skowls, you knew about Falco's experiment and *you let this happen!"* Raydo unclasped his hand and stared into her from the hollowed socket. *"Can you fix this?* Shake your body and make it better? No. And *what is your magical sexiness going to do about our crops?"*

Claudio looked down at Zayger, still huddled on the ground, her head bobbing in shame. "Zayger, the hunters - *don't explain anything*, just make sure they're alright. GO. Shayra, see to the gardeners and the harvest." The teenagers ran out of the glade. "Raydo--"

Raydo swiped his blade from the ground and sprang, pressing it against Claudio's neck. "You'd be dead right now if I thought you knew." His arm, tense and quivering, loosened and lowered the knife. "But you don't. And your blood won't heal the fields from this." Again he turned and advanced on Balya. "It's *you.* Kayno is Kayno, Falco is Falco, *you're supposed to be priestess of Deia – you betrayed us!"*

Claudio clasped him from behind, lifting the teenager's feet from the ground. *"That's enough. You're coming with me."*

"Put him down," the priestess' voice shook the trees. "A tested hunter will not be lifted like a child. Raydo..."

"Back off. I can find Ayma on my own." and he staggered off toward the village.

♭

Bayla looked at Claudio, his gaze far away, alone somewhere, his heavy cheeks and forehead hanging like stone slabs. She put a finger to her lips and touched a scorched crater on his arm. He winced but didn't pull away. She touched a burn on his chest, wishing she could fall into him but afraid that he would crumble. His stare returned from the distance, no less grim but a little warmer. Lifting on his toes, he gently touched his forehead to hers.

"The harvest is ruined," Shayra said, softly approaching, "What we buried is safe, but it won't get us through winter, and first frost is tonight."

"The gardeners?" Bayla asked.

"Yes, the women and children will be fine, but we'll need a lot of skins to mend holes in the tents."

Zayger shuffled in and mumbled, "Leather patches, that's all we'll get from what we've hunted... All melted and poisoned... But the Feast of First Frost, Zayger...will..."

"Zayger," the priestess shook her head, lowly.

Claudio's face hung again. "The animals have gone to ground."

Shayra looked at Bayla, "We could send messengers to the other tribes."

Now Bayla stared into the distance, "The skowls will have passed over them too."

ß

"Bayla," Shayra stepped forward, "Talk to the spirits. Tell them we're not ready for winter. Another half moon."

"Are *you* ready? You had the vision."

"You...you hid this from me. And now it's *my* responsibility? Look at what your secret has done!"

"Did I send you the vision? Did I put the skowls in your mind seven moons ago? *You are chosen, not by me, by the spirits.* This crisis calls to *you*. Will you answer? Bayla."

"No, don't call me that."

"Bayla. It's who you are."

"No!" Shayra shouted and ran from the clearing.

ß

Bayla watched her go, then centered her body for a slow, mournful dance. "Mother land, father sky... You lead the seasonal circle-dance and the children follow. But the music begins and we are not ready. Will you slow the tune?"

Bayla and Claudio stood still, peering out into the forest as if it might speak in response. But there was no word, only the cold whistle of an icy wind. They shivered. Claudio sighed, then nodded and spoke to the ground. "You need to go, start mending the tent. My old uniform, it'll be hard to cut but the patches will be strong, share them in the village."

"Come with me."

"You know I can't."

Raydo lumbered into the glade, wearing a leather eyepatch and carrying two spears. "Kayno I'm sorry."

"You were right. And you're right again. We hunt." Claudio reached out and the young hunter tossed him a spear. "We'll be back in three days with whatever we can catch."

Bayla said "The frost is coming *tonight.*"

Zayger, brightened at the prospect of a hunt, drew her knife. "Zayger's gonna make a snufallo sleeping-bag. Hope they don't smell as bad on the *inside* as--"

Raydo brushed her aside, "There *is* no Zayger, you *have* no name. Go away."

These cold words and their clear effect on the huntress gave Claudio an icy twist inside, but he had no warmth to offer. "Tell the married men to go home, anyone else can volunteer. I'll be right behind you," he said to Raydo, who stalked off toward the stream. Falco and Donna stepped into the clearing, but Claudio kept his eyes steady on Balya. "Here we are."

"Here we are," she said, taking his hands.

"I'll miss you."

"You'll die."

Claudio sighed grimly and looked at Falco. "That's what I'm good for."

"Take *this* with you." She stepped up, enclosed and kissed him, trying to breathe some heat into his body.

Falco approached him as well. "Here, take this too."

"...Your *toy?*"

"In case you forget what a real man is."

Passing into Claudio's tense hand tripped the action figure's speech-button. "Somebody light my cigarillo before it...crawls away."

"I'll never forget the kind of 'real man' *you* are."

Donna breathlessly said, "*Nobody* can..."

Claudio shook his head in disgust and walked off after Raydo.

ʓ

Bayla's eyes longingly followed Claudio into the scorched forest, out of sight. Falco assumed a trophy pose, and respectfully waited. A cold breeze blew by, rustling the wind-chime of dangled beads in her hair and corset. Falco's black pleated skirt fluttered reverently. "I guess you'll be happy to know my crop was completely destroyed."

She turned to him and squinted. "Why would that make me happy?"

"I...just thought..."

"I'm happy that you're safe. And you're welcome here with us. Winter rolls in fast and supplies are short, but we'll share what we have."

"The Interstellar Syndicate does not accept charity. Rescue is coming, maybe not till spring but I'll explain the situation, they'll take care of your bird problem."

Donna stepped forward. "Also your shampoo problem."

"You won't have to worry about food."

Bayla eyed them, quizically. "But we *weren't* worried about food."

"In the meantime I volunteer to personally

commandeer this situation. Willing, of course, to make concessions to some of your savage customs – if you people believe that dancing solves everything? You are fortunate to have a three-time Tina-Turner-Award-winning private dancer at your disposal. Any old music will do, even this bongo-circle crap you listen to here."

Donna helpfully interjected, "That won't be necessary – I can build an 8-bit synthesizer from the pod's control circuits."

"I can teach you a tango, forbidden, from the brothels of Buenos Aires that may very well somehow solve this hunger problem. Combining our abilities, you and I will get this village through this crisis... What?"

Bayla's overcast features had brightened, and her musical laughter harmonized with a jangle of beads. "I'm sorry, Calvin, please do continue..."

"You don't believe I can fix this."

"Actually I do. I really do. If you say that you and I having sex right here, right now will somehow produce enough food for the tribe to live comfortably all winter? If *you* say it? *I believe* it."

"Oh. So, um..?"

"And it's *still* not going to happen. Calvin. There is a crisis. We will live or die. As Deians."

♭

Donna lightly touched Falco's shoulder. "Captain, I've been observing here six months. These creatures won't respond to reason. I invoke Syndicate proposition four fifty-one."

"The crew extracts the captain's head from his

own ass? But that's only to be invoked in a *literal* sense. *And* it requires that the crew outnumber the captain."

"You've given this hunter honorary status. Are you with us?"

Zayger had made herself so small that Falco forgot she was there. "I...don't know..."

"Yes, you do." Donna clamped her shoulders and lifted her, setting the huntress down solid on her feet. "You invent yourself, regardless of what others plan for you. You determine who you are. And when your identity-quest hits limits in one place? That's what the galaxy is for. And *that* is what the Syndicate is for."

Zayger's face turned toward Bayla, then snapped back and looked Donna in the eye. "I'm in. ...But how do we get head from the Captain? From his ass, I mean..?"

"We are members of the Interstellar Syndicate. We live and die by the Prime Elective: *'Do What You've Gotta Do.'* You can't make an omelet without replicating some egg-like substance. Right now our pan is a broken pod, our I-can't-believe-it's-like-butter is a champion skrote-snatcher and--"

"Also I can bend my finger back this far--"

"Our egg-white is a super-sexy navigratrix who got perfect scores on *all* her academic *and* physical exams. Also she holds the academy hula-hoop record. *Six. Days.* Hm? *And,* drum-roll?"

Zayger patted rhythmically on her abdomen.

"And our golden yolk is that dashing-est, daring-est, most published captain in Syndicate history, Calvin Theseus Falco. The man who *always* comes out on top. And deep inside I *believe* he will come out on top of this omelet, no matter how messy it gets. Captain. We're *with* you."

Falco wiped away a tear. "Lieutenant, that was...incredible. If you weren't a woman I would kiss you. Or if you were some *other* woman."

Donna involuntarily grimaced, then brightened. "We've got work to do."

Falco nodded. "Engage."

They strode out into the woods, Zayger turning back a moment to steal a glance at Bayla's green eyes. The priestess nodded respectfully.

ᛉ

Bayla closed her eyes and hummed low, spreading her arms for a slow, meditative dance. She squatted and swiveled, palms gliding over the wounded grasses and moss. Then the corner of her lip curled into a smile as she picked up the familiar musk of Ayma, laboriously lurching into the glade, bell-beads tolling low and calm.

The priestess stood, and bent slightly so the old woman could whisper something into her ear. Bayla laughed long and loud, breaking into a goose-step dance. Then she wrapped her arms around Ayma and kissed the top of her mushroom hood.

Ayma whispered again and Bayla turned serious. "*No.* He will die at the appointed time."

The old woman bowed reverently.

Shayra stepped into the glade, beads tinkling timidly. "I'm sorry."

"We change at our own pace," Bayla said.

Ayma nodded, and Shayra kissed her hood. "Here we are. Three, and one."

Turning inward they took hands in a circle. Humming a chord together, they curled inward toward the blue ground and bloomed outward toward the green sky, then inward toward the ground again.

Ring Seal, Crete, c1500BCE

THIRTEENTH MOON

Seven moons had waxed and waned since the skowl attack.

For three moons the land had lain dark and quiet, healing under a blanket of heavy snow.

Then a moon of thaw brought on the soupy season of primordial muck and mist.

This was followed by three moons of lengthening days when the strengthening sun baked the forest floor and bare trees bedazzled themselves with fronds of many shapes and shades to attract its rays. The forest's fertility pageant attained its full pitch in gaudy colors and dusky smells, lewd bird-songs and crude creature-calls. Trees voluptuously jutted their fruits, bushes unabashedly hung their berries and flowers flagrantly splayed their vulgar organs.

"Peet? Peet Peet?" a curlibird's chirp flicked through the purple forest.

A gurlibird on a nearby tree poked her head out of an animal carcass and peered around, then looked downward at the eggs she'd laid inside it. She shook her head. "Noot."

The curlibird processed this information and reconsidered its approach. "...Poot?"

After another glance at her cache of eggs, the gurlibird shrugged her wings, puffed her breast-feathers and responded: "*Re*peet."

13

With a low tolling of beads the crooked, mushroom-hooded figure shuffled into the glade. She sniffed around, then pulled up a pipe and dug into a pouch for a pinch of tree-bark to fill it. Humming a low note she waited, a buzzing alerted her to the approach of an insect and she hummed till it was within reach. Then she snapped out her arm and caught it between long fingers. Cracking it in two produced a spark and she inhaled deeply from the pipe.

A crackle of twigs, Falco had stepped into the clearing. Not a wrinkle in his grey uniform, not a hair out of place, trademarked jaw still smooth and sharp as the day he'd graduated from the academy. He approached her cautiously, leaned in, and she exhaled a fog of blue smoke into his face. "Do you know who I am?"

Falco coughed. "Do *you* know who you are? This smells pretty strong."

"I am the waning moonshiner, listener of the spirits."

"You're the famous Ayma."

"And you're the famous Falco."

"Well. 'Famous Falco' might be a little...redundant. You may call me Captain."

The old woman stood motionless. Then she burst into laughter – low at first like the tolling of her beads, then rising into a high cackle that sent cold flashes through his lower spine. Laughing harder she gasped, heaved, and collapsed on the ground. Silence descended on the glade.

Falco nudged her with his boot but she didn't move. "So, um. Pleasure to finally meet you." He turned to go.

"Help me up, child?" She said, and Falco extended a hand. "I'm sorry. Hearing you say 'Captain' made me think of something funny. And what did you say you were captain of?"

"My ship? You're sitting in it."

"Oh? Give it a good rinse before you put it on again."

"This planet."

"Is a starship?"

"If it's moving through space and it's got Falco on it, then it must be my ship."

"Well treat her gently, young man. Like a lady - you don't want to get her pummeled to death like your last ship."

"You...know about--"

"One does not have to be blind to see *your* situation. I hear things..."

"The trees..." Falco peered around suspiciously.

She patted his muscular thigh reassuringly. "The trees don't need to obsess about you. They only fear the grain and the sands below. I hear legends of Captain Falco, riding his beautiful killer, the shuttle Exogamy. I heard you one day fornicated with voluptuous octopus octuplets..."

"It takes mathematical precision."

"And then motorcycle magazine-model triplets in detroit?"

"It takes engineering precision."

"...And? Is it true, the legend of that day?" She took a long slow pull from her pipe.

"...Well. You left out the parts where I saved octo-planet from the evil doctor Skun-*jee*li...and revived Detroit's industrial techno scene. *And* when writing about that day I left out the hours in between, when I diffused a pewtron bomb and then rode off into the sunset on a swervey astro-physicist. That was personal. But yes, then it was back to work. There's always a planet to save."

ß

"Are you going to save this world?"

"Hey, look. I think it's great that you're old and wasted and people pay attention to you. I really respect that. But these primitive savages here don't know about schools, where one in every five children can learn to read. They're growing up without pagers, telescreens and a hundred other devices to cure us of human interaction. And these kids have never known the unconditional love and infinite forgiveness of Santa Claus and the Easter Bunny, who give trinkets and candy no matter how naughty you are. And *you* wouldn't need to... I guess your job isn't that strenuous, but you could be in a well-lit antiseptic facility. Fluorescent lights? White tile? Perfection. They don't allow smoking? But I'll disable the bathroom detector for you."

"I don't know what a 'bath-room' is but it's very kind of you to offer."

"Women *love* it there. They come back? Feeling so much prettier. You'll think you died and went to porcelain paradise."

"And if we refuse to worship your porcelain god--"

"*Everybody* bows down to the porcelain god."

She puffed again. "What's important is that you genuinely want to share something."

"We're not so different, you and I. In most ways? Absolutely. But in a couple small ways we're... We both put the people around us first."

"Don't the people around *you* usually...*die* first? And don't you then emerge unscathed, not one hair out of place?" She extended a hand.

"Don't. Touch. The hair. You have *no* idea how hard it is to maintain this look while living in a tree."

"How can you call yourself a savior when everything around you gets dramatically destroyed?"

"I've saved more lives than Rock & Roll."

"Who have you saved here? These people should have spent the winter in their huts eating and humping, but instead they've been scraping fallen trees and crunching insects because *you* brought destruction. And your starship crew...smashed to space-dust. But here *you* are."

Falco's lips and eyelids tightened. "*I* didn't ask to be dragged off the ship. We all knew the risk, that's part of the mission."

"But *who* knew the mission? What *was* the mission?"

♭

Falco looked around, the forest was still and insects were chirping. He shrugged. "I guess there's no way anything *you* say would stand up in space-court. A little over a year ago I was called into a meeting. A transmission from Venus demanded that the Syndicate hand me over..."

"As a criminal."

"What..? No, as an ambassador. Of modern dance. And judge of intergalactic fertility pageants. I told those faceless bureaucrats there must be some mix-up – 'Ambassador?' I'm the *badass*-itor. Finally old chancellor chrome-dome and I came to an agreement... I would take my laser-pistol out of his nostril, and he would send me on a tippity-top-secret double-dog dare squared classified mission - steal the Exogamy and go rogue, braving an asteroid field to sabotage an enemy t-shirt manufacture colony. If I survived I'd be disgraced, disqualified from ambassadorship...stripped of rank, sent back to the academy. Last time I made captain in five years, *this* time I'll do it in three."

Ayma wheezed another cloud of smoke into Falco's face. "They sent you off to die," her voice crackled.

Falco coughed and fanned the smoke away. "They knew I'd make it."

"But you *didn't* make it. You got everybody killed, your crew--"

"No I fired my classic crew beforehand. Officer Sprickett, Doctor McCohen, Dutchie? Replaced them with extras..."

"Your ship was destroyed."

"We were speeding through the asteroids, old-school break-beat maneuvers. And a call came in... Would I defend my title on a Japanese game-show? And I wondered...can I still eat that many shrimp...while arm-wrestling a naughty schoolteacher *and* a tentacle-monster? For a moment I...hesitated... Then I said '*yes*' and an asteroid bashed off a rear engine...my beautiful Exogamy... Destroyed. One year ago today..." Falco's body had swept into a sculpture stance of longing toward the sky, his black pleated skirt billowed in mourning.

♭3

The hunched, hooded figure straightened her spine triumphantly. "I *knew* it. I'd heard that there must be some crack, some weakness, some gooey center under all that musk and muscle and smarmy machismo. But I didn't want to believe it, had to find out for myself. And here you are, every inch a man, you're the one..."

"*That's* what I've been trying to *tell* everybody all year, but--" Falco recoiled as she pulled her robes open. "Hey, cut that out. Falco doesn't...boldly go there..."

"You are the one." With the clanking of large beads, Ayma's heavy tendriled robes fell to the ground.

"And you are out of your mind, and need to get back *into* reality and your clothes."

Her body was not what Falco expected – it was curvy and strong, hips and breasts that looked weaponized in a white swimsuit and shiny thigh-high black boots. A conical bustier and corset arsenal, gun-belt around her narrow waist and ammunition cartridges strapped to her muscular arms. The word "Assassin" printed across her broad bottom. Having shed the robes she stood to her full height, nearly as tall as the Captain, and tossed aside the mushroom-like hood. Her face was sharp, angular cheekbones and thin wide lips, platinum hair sleeked back, eyes hidden behind mirrored triangle sunglasses.

"Captain Falco," she said in a different voice, still low but younger.

"Wow," he squinted, "I think I got a...contact buzz off whatever you're smoking..."

ʓ

"Do you know who I am?" She asked, an eyebrow peaking above her angular sunglasses. The eyebrow was black, and sharp.

Falco blinked, perplexed. "You're an old blind witchdoctor and I'm hallucinating that you're a sexy sci-fi space-babe."

"Athena Kernikovia. Your new collection officer."

Falco nodded, this did make sense. Then he tensed. "You...you killed the famous Ayma."

"I've been here two weeks, studying Ayma, and these Deians. It was time to kill her this morning, and as I walked up she asked me why. I told her my employers have big plans for Captain Falco and she...started cackling...laughed herself to death..."

"Well. So it goes. But what are we standing around for? Here is my head - put a bag over it and return me to the Syndicate at once."

"That's right, you haven't heard. The Syndicate sunk. In a catastrophic flood of unpaid air-conditioning bills. Federation Loan foreclosed, the Interstellar Syndicate is now a subsidiary. We own the Syndicate, your contract, your merchandizing rights. And your jaw-line, registered trademark."

"*...What?*" Falco said, more to test the jaw than anything else.

"Captain, you were six billion spacebucks in academic debt. *Before* the Exogamy crashed, and you became responsible for the student loans of everyone aboard. That makes nearly *seven* billion. We bought you out. We've got bigger plans for you."

"...'Bigger'? What could possibly be bigger than Captain Falco in an intergalactic series of episodic conquests? Adventure, romance, life-lessons, collectibles? Launching subterranean mouth-breathers into endless technical debates?"

"I've got one-and-a-half words for you... Falco-topia."

"...No, I think it's only one word, that's what I called the back seat of my first Chevy."

"Yes, and we *have* that Chevy. We've found everything, spent the last year collecting. Oriana's chastity belt. The Golden Fleece with the black collar. Ursula Major's bikini."

"Wow... Where did you find *that?*"

"Ebay."

"Must have been a fierce auction."

"Not when you can send drone-assassins after other bidders. And all of it will be yours again. Here. In Falco-topia, registered theme-park. RPG rated NCC-seventeen-o-*one?* Polka-tonk? Kari-yodel-oki?" She pulled a small plastic cup from a holster. "Falco-tility clinic? A full-scale model of the Exogamy with an all-you-can-eat kick-line buffet? And Falco himself in five hundred panel-discussions a year."

"But that's impossible. I'm *not* some piece of Captain Falco memorabilia – *I am Captain Falco.* I belong *out there*, beyond the rim of star-light--"

"You belong to Federation Loan." She held

up a little finger. It was sharp. "And I am authorized to get your pinky-swear by any means necessary."

"I'll tell you where you can stick my pinky-finger."

Athena glanced around furtively, then leaned. "...Serious?"

"No, forget that. I'll tell you where you can*not* put my pinky-finger. Because I refuse. This planet has a greater value – naïve natives, rich topsoil? As an agricultural colony--"

"You haven't seen this planet from space. Ninety-eight percent of the landmass is desert."

"But...it's so *alive* here..."

"Yes, this was a forest world. But two hundred years ago a Syndicate transport crash-landed here, the long-lost...Thomas Jefferson Starship."

"No, that was cloud-busted by the Golden Girls, I wrote a midterm paper, got an A++ with fifteen stickers--"

"I've seen the wreckage and found the captain's journal."

ß

Athena pulled a small, battered cassette player from her belt. She pressed play, and a man's voice crackled from its tiny speaker. "Dear Syndicate diary. It's been twenty-nine years since we crash-landed here. The clean air and water, bountiful fruits and intoxicants have had an alarming effect on my crew...and the women's hockey teams we were transporting to playoffs. The *planet itself*...is an aphrodisiac, our population quickly quintupled...the lion's share of blame is mine. So we started torching forest, farming barley, leaving desert in our wake. And then came the skowls... Today we voted to split up into seven separate groups and live primitive in what's left of the woodland. This is my last Dear Syndicate Diary entry, I will wander the woods alone, overseeing the transition. Your friend, Captain Bill Hollocks."

Falco's registered trademark jaw was hanging slack. His eyes had turned from green to blue. He winced in pain envisioning stickers being peeled from his academy midterm paper like bandages from a wound. *Then* he realized some of his conclusions about Deia had been faulty. He gasped. "What--"

The recording resumed: "PS – you may commence...crying for me *now*, Argentina."

A wave of emotion gripped Falco's abdomen as he realized that Bill Hollocks, *the* Bill Hollocks, legendary moonwalker, fearless hairstyle pioneer, textbook hero, Captain William "the Specimen" Hollocks, had died here. And his bones were somewhere in the soil of Deia.

♭

Falco resumed his composure. "...And the other groups? Let me guess. Jam-banded themselves to death?"

"There are still seven tribes here, similar to the one you've met. They have their separate territories and play out silly little panty-raids and war-games every few years when the genes get thin. These are human beings, Captain. They've been waiting eight generations for rescue, they may not even remember that they're waiting anymore."

"They're *people...* If I'd known I would have...*laughed* at them more..."

"It's time we return them to civilization."

"What, so they can be carnies in your amusement park?"

"Of course not, their primitive stone-age diet has made them much too tall for that. We'll transport them to one of the refugee planets and rehabilitate them there. Except for this magnificent priestess who stays here with you."

Falco smirked. "Ha. Hey, when you try to convince her of that – can I watch?"

"She'll be here. Either by choice, or stuffed and mounted."

"This is..." the Captain sputtered, his head spinning. "But the Prime Elective!"

"There *is* no Prime Elective. *'Do What You've Gotta Do'* is over. The Syndicate is gone. Now the only rule is *'Do What We Tell You.'* And we're telling you now. Falco-topia is *happening*. Here."

"You can't..."

"But *you* can. You're Calvin Theseus Falco. You can't lose. Deliver the terms. Assimilation? Or annihilation. You see these hands? They're..." Her hands, like sharp weapons, had risen. She stared at them a moment, then waved one in front of her face. "These hands are...really...big... Too big! Get back!" She pulled her hands behind her and looked desperately at Falco. "No one told me my hands were that big. What's happening to me?"

"You're stoned."

"No! I've been vaccinated, every known drug

in the universe. But I... My hands... I can't hear my hands. Can you hear my hands?"

"Get your hands *away* from the hair, I won't tell you again."

"I need to... I need to lie down. Power-nap. When I get back...Captain Falco will have this situation under control. Or these hands start...singing-- killing..." She hobbled off into the forest, unaware of Ayma's robes and hood trailing, hooked on one of her boots.

ᛉ

Falco cast his two-thousand-lightyear stare into the sky, assimilating this new information.

Claudio entered the glade. "Captain..?"

"Ensign."

"What are you doing here?"

"Same thing I do *everywhere*. Make the human race look *good*."

"You have to leave. Now."

"I am *not* one of your bongo-drumming jungle hippies."

"Raydo's coming--" Darting a glance back into the forest, Claudio urgently stepped toward Falco and pressed his shoulder.

The Captain was firm as a statue. "Have you ever seen a Pretzelon ballerina twist both feet into her nostrils?" He landed his cold gaze on Claudio. "That's what you will look like if you don't take your hand off me."

Claudio stepped back. "Captain. *Please*."

Falco stared him up and down. He looked older, deep lines had cut themselves into his brow.

Scars from the skowl-droppings were brown and shiny against his gold skin and blue facepaint. His marshmallow cheeks were now leathery and caved, and his eyes were ringed with crackles and darkness. Claudio's hair was a mane of shiny curls, now streaked with white, and a full rack of antlers jutted from his forehead. This was no longer an ensign, and Falco realized with some dismay that there was no reason anymore except appeasement for this man to say "Captain" or "Please."

"Well," Falco said, adjusting the tuck of his uniform shirt. "Because you said *both* of the magic words." Claudio led and Falco followed to a nearby spot where they crouched in the brush.

ß

A gloomy figure lurched into the glade, wearing a hood and long cloak of sharp black feathers. He carried a makeshift metal crossbow and peered around suspiciously with one eye, the other obscured by a leather mask covering a side of his face. He sniffed the air.

Falco's eyes widened - this grim and muscular killer had been that boy, the young hunter, Raydo. But the bandy-limbed laddy was barely recognizable in this tree-trunk solid warrior. He even seemed taller, though there was no way he could have grown this much in half a year, it was a change in his posture from low ranging darts to forward indestructible strides. No response to the tinkling of beads as Shayra stepped into the clearing behind him. He sniffed the air again.

"Ayma was just *here*. Why?"

Shayra smiled.   "...Besides being old and blind and stoned?"

"There's something else too. A force I haven't smelled since... *Falco!*" He whipped an arrow from a sheath at his thigh and cranked it into the crossbow, taking his first heavy step toward where Falco and Claudio were hiding.

"Raydo *stop.*" Shayra gripped his shoulder.

"He's *here.*" Raydo pulled.

Shayra tried to sweep his feet out from under him but it didn't work.

"I don't want to play! I've tracked the last of the skowls to a cave. I only came to forge more arrows."

"Look at me!" Her shout echoed through the trees. Raydo stiffened, then slowly turned to face her. He had not looked her in the eye since the Skowl attack. He thought at first she'd been crying but realized there was an acid scar running down her cheek like a tear. A cruel and hungry winter had cut some creases into her dark skin, but the weathering only made her eyes shine brighter.   She had broadened slightly as well, her stance was stronger and more confident, her figure fuller despite months of privation. When she spoke, he noticed that even her voice had deepened, broadened, gained a new gravity.   "The ancient Bollox thought it was perfecting the world. And it killed off many breeds of creature. It was a criminal."

Raydo tried to smile at her, the leather mask resisted. It had been seven moons since he'd smiled. "Shayra, the *skowls* - we barely survived the winter. And they'll keep coming, long as Spaceman Spiff keeps farming his barley."

"The skowls are part of this balance – do we have the wisdom to decide their kind shouldn't live?"

Raydo pulled back his hood to give her a full view of the mask. *"Look at me."*

She winced, shrinking a moment, not from fear but sadness. Then regained her full height. "I *have*, I *do*, I *will*. From our infancy till the end. I'll never turn away from you. And to me you'll always be--"

"That's not who I am anymore. The Captain and the skowls..."

"They hurt you but only *you* can change who you are...melting metal? Using this...*thing*..?"

"It's *called* a Rayd-bow. I made it so we could hunt creatures that fly."

"But you're *not* 'hunting.' You hunt to feed the tribe - *now* you're just... Just *killing*."

*"Some*body needs to save our people," he grunted, turning away.

"Yes. But why can't that 'somebody' be Raydo? Whatever Falco and skowls crap down on us, I could say 'well? Here we are...' But if *you* destroy the man I love..."

Raydo hung his head. Then he turned to her again and she gripped him firmly, pulled his face to hers and kissed him, hard.

When she released him Raydo breathed heavy, mouth and eyes open wide. "It's happened."

"I know," she said, solemnly.

"Bayla...here you are."

"The Thirteenth Moon."

"The Bollox hunt."

"It's time," she said. "It's *our* time."

"It's our time."

"I'll go tell Ayma."

"I'll sharpen my spear," he gazed out into the deep, dank purple forest. "The Bollox deserves a clean kill." He lumbered in one direction, she stepped in the other. Then both stopped, turned and lunged into each others' arms again. For a long moment they gripped, an embrace so powerful they they might have been a tree. Then they unclasped and sprinted to their tasks.

ᛦ

Falco and Claudio emerged into the glade.

"What are *you* smiling about?" Falco glanced sideways. "Sounds like he wants your job."

Claudio nodded, grinning. "If he's ready? He can have it. These antlers *do* get heavy."

Falco laughed. Claudio laughed. They laughed a moment, together.

But the Captain stiffened to command posture when Donna and Zayger entered the glade, wearing crude Syndicate uniforms patched from skins and fronds. Falco nodded to Donna.

"Captain, the leaves are dry, humidity is right."

"We dug the rest of the trenches, it's time for...the fire..." Zayger blushed, timidly meeting Claudio's gaze. "Kayno."

"Hang on a moment," Falco said, leading Donna a few yards into the forest for a status update.

ᛦ

Claudio breathed a heavy sigh. Despite his feelings about it, the huntress looked perfectly natural and happy in the makeshift uniform. The grass skirt looked strange on her, but the boxy patchwork shirt and leather armband with its crude Syndicate insignia were lovingly done and appeared comfortable. "Zayger. You're..."

"That's the *old* me. The Captain gave me a new name... Keefer. Keefer *Suth*erlander."

Claudio felt a warm smile break over his face. "I'm...sure you've earned it..."

"How's Raydo? And the others?"

"Raydo's been... I've barely seen him around the village and he never speaks. When I see smoke from his foundry I ask for advice, but he won't answer. The village mourns him. It's been a hard winter. But tonight is Thirteenth Moon and tomorrow morning..."

Her gaze drifted off through the purple fronds and leaves, into the depths of the forest. "Hunting season..."

"Won't be the same without Zayger."

"Somebody *else* will have to be the best. I mean besides *me*, off wherever I am."

"What have you put in your hair?"

"Don't touch the hair. We've been experimenting, but the academy has hair-technicians and once I've enlisted--"

"The academy?" Claudio's teeth clenched. "Falco..."

"He's writing me a letter of recommendation." She pulled out a strip of leather.

"Let me see that. This is an *open* letter. It says 'Dear women of Earth. Do us all a favor. Put on ten pounds. Sincerely, your friend Captain Falco.'"

"I know, it's good advice. He hasn't written *mine* yet, he said I could hold onto this and practice my reading. But the Captain's bold, strident prose is going to win me a discount for a bachelor of security-officer arts."

"...You know what *happens* to security officers..? All the time..."

"They swear to protect the captain and Syndicate properties, though it may entail gruesome death by incineration, mastication, depilitation--"

"I know the oath. But is that really what you want?"

"None of that's gonna happen to *me*. I'm young and idealistic. People like that *never* die tragically in space adventures."

"Zayger--"

She snatched the letter and pulled away. "That's not my name anymore."

"But you *earned* it, you were so *proud* of it."

"*You* were a Syndicate officer named Claudio. *Kayno*. You strode into our lives, a submissive man in a skirt. *Now* you're nothing but a virile buck."

"I...won't argue with that. But you *know* me, we've hunted together."

"But *you never told me* about Brazil. The beautiful Bauhaus architecture, Krautrock, Fahrvegnügen on stocky fraulines, fun-fun-fun on the Autobahn. We could have that *here*. The Captain says, once I've set up some digital identity accounts, he and I can be friends in so many ways - we won't even need to *see* each other again. And festivals like the Thirteenth moon? They do that every night in a thousand night-clubs. And friends like Raydo? On

Earth they call them 'jack-wads'? Coffee-shops are *swarming* with them."

"I'm *from* Earth. People there would sell their digital *souls* to be part of what you were born into *here*."

"'Here' is too small for people like the Captain and me, who make our *own* destiny. I chase my fate like I chase my dinner." Having involuntarily sunk into a hunter's crouch, she jerked her posture back into Syndicate stance.

"You know there's no meat on Earth, or aboard any starship. It's all ground-up meal-worms fed on styrofoam."

"Donna-tennant says a high-styrofoam diet helps to keep Syndicate personnel afloat during tsunami season. And if I ever miss the hunt? There's a magic rabbit, drops chocolatey pellets on Easter? I haven't told the Captain, but I think if I stayed up *really* late..."

"People have tried that before."

"People. But not *Zayger*-- I mean...*Keefer*..."

ꝋ

Donna and Falco walked back into the glade. "So *what* is there to think about?" She turned her face from Falco to Claudio. "Status update. Captain Falco will be taking over the planet in this next nineteen minutes. Starting...now."

Claudio squinted. "Um, sorry I...missed that whole scene you two were playing up there."

Donna flashed him a stare of mild annoyance. "Haven't you ever heard of 'eavesdropping?'"

Zayger joined, enthusiastically. "Like when

you chase a jackanape into a tree? And you look up? And he... Wait - what does *that* have to do with *this?* What's happening?"

"Take a deep breath... Falco-topia."

Claudio rolled his eyes, "Here we go."

Zayger darted her head eagerly, "Is it a sauce? A delicious Falco-sauce?"

"No, it's like *U*topia, except it's *him*-topia – *Falco*-topia. Federation Loan is sponsoring Captain Falco the amusement park. So?" She raised an eyebrow at Claudio. "We're on a schedule here – you gonna fight him or what?"

He squinted, puzzled. "No."

"He's already beaten you anyway. Check. Time to enlighten the priestess and process the villagers."

Falco had been oddly silent. Zayger hopped over to him. "Captain, what about the Syndicate? The academy?"

Donna sighed, "Yes, yes, panel discussion to follow. Right now we need to get this revolution started."

Claudio jutted his jaw. "'Revolution'? This is not a change in a soft-drink recipe, it's-- We're talking about the end of a sustainable alien culture.

"Oh, that's right, you missed the plot-twist. They're not aliens."

"No, because this is *their world* – *we're* the alien invaders--"

"No I mean they're from Earth, hotshots and hockey-players, stranded here after a crash. Why are the women here so beefy and hairy? Now we know. Look. We can do the whole 'big reveal' and geek out about it later but right now we've got to--"

"Lieutenant," Falco interrupted sternly. "Cool your jets."

ƀ

Falco was in one of his statue postures, the introspective one, and after interjecting he gave everyone a moment to reposition themselves around him. Finally Zayger broke the silence. "Captain."

He smirked, wearily. "I would say that 'the grown-ups need to talk,' but..." Looking at Claudio he couldn't help but laugh. "You...just look so *ridiculous* in that costume..."

Claudio sighed. "Well I'm glad we had this chance to...connect."

"But seriously," Falco wiped away a tear and got serious. "How's this gonna play out?"

Claudio's jaw dropped. He stuttered helplessly, trying to get the words out. "What..? *You're* Captain Falco and you're asking--"

"A human coat-rack, I know--"

"*You* tell *me*. Because if there's one thing I know about you it's that Falco doesn't lose. So *what* is *Falco* going to *do?*"

"What does Calvin want?" The forest shook with Bayla's voice as she strode into the clearing.

Falco's body jerked, startled. "*Wow. You* need to start calling ahead to warn people because *you walk in* and all the blood leaves my brain. I was confused enough already--"

Donna snarled, "She won't need to call ahead after reconditioning...by taxidermy."

"*Taxidermy?*" Claudio jolted.

"Falco's last trophy, alive or dead."

"Lieutenant." Falco snapped at her.

ß

Falco tried to resume his thoughtful, heroic stance but his limbs and joints all felt out of place. Bayla's presence, once again, had changed the whole balance of the scene, his body, his thoughts, everything. She was so broad, everywhere he tried to look, she was there. And something like a personal gravity surrounded her, everything seemed to swirl in her orbit. Plus, seeing her in this new light, descended from hockey champions and Syndicate officers, maybe even the great Captain Bill Hollocks himself, introduced a whole new frontier of gnawing curiosity.

"Well?" she demanded.

Falco cleared his throat but his mind was blank. "I... We..."

She sniffed. "There's an unfamiliar scent on the air. What manner of monster comes hunting the famous Falco?"

Donna nimbly inserted herself between them. "Someone's been sent to rescue us. And *you*. From all this."

"...And what part of 'all this' do I look like I need rescue from?"

"Seriously..? If I had three mouths talking at once it would take all day."

"If you had three mouths talking at once I'd *know* what I needed rescue from. But *aside* from that--"

"We have new information."

"A shocking twist indeed. That all along I've

been a damsel in distress, desperately holding out for a hero in a skirt."

Falco attempted to regain control. "*Look,* this...*you*...the Collector... Lieutenant, *stand down.* Everybody, just..."

Bayla leaned in heavily at him. "What's *wrong,* Calvin? It's what you wanted. Ever since crash-landing a year ago today you've been lost. We deviated from your formula of episodic conquests, you were afraid the space-time continuum would *collapse* unless an exotic space-babe fell into your arms and the natives chanted your name. So? Here at last, the stars realign, the universe settles back on its axis, revolving around Falco. The exotic enchantress is yours, apparently, and she is asking you – *what does Calvin want?"*

"I..."

"WHAT DOES CALVIN WANT?"

Falco fell backward, the ground thudding against his shoulders.

Donna dove down, "Captain!" She lifted him, but his legs wouldn't take his weight. "What have you *done* to him?"

"I asked him a question. I don't have any 'alien' powers."

Claudio squinted. "You know about that..?"

ʒ

"I inherited the secret when I became priestess, yes. But it makes no difference where our ancestors were born. *We're from here.* The forests of Deia have mothered us, raised us, teach us who we are. We're members of *this living community.* We *can't* be that somewhere else."

Donna squinted. "You can be *human* somewhere else. You live like animals here."

"Living like animals is our favorite part of being human."

"But you could have so much *more*. Machines – friendly, reliable washing machines and seductive automobiles, enthusiastic power-tools. All you need your hands for? Grappling with nineteen remote controls."

Zayger stepped up cheerfully, "There's something called 'auto-erotic asphyxiation,' and some people enjoy it so much they *die*."

Falco grimaced. "*And* some people survive, but that's not--"

"Look," Claudio said, "You're right, Earth has all kinds of *stuff*. But the people of Deia *must* have a choice."

Donna laughed again. "*Wow*, you said 'must.' Your *majesty*. How could they choose when they don't *know* what they're missing? Sponge-candy. Vanilla Ice. Segways."

The priestess remained calm. "We know what we *have* and it *works*."

"Maybe it just works for *you* and that's why you're so afraid of change."

"Change is constant and fear won't stop it. The events set in motion when you landed here will settle tonight. Something will end, something will begin. That's the way of it. Only one thing is unexpected here. Calvin."

He looked up, the weight of her stare heavy on his shoulders. "...What?"

"Falco is looking for *you*." She advanced, he

retreated.

"...No, you're confused – *Federation Loan* sent a *Collections Officer* because *my fans*--"

"I understand it perfectly. Falco the *brand* is looking for Falco the *man*. And? What does Calvin want?"

"You don't know what the Collector is capable of--"

"But I know what *you're* capable of. Emerging from any species of disaster untouched, your flawless jaw, your perfect hair--"

He'd stepped backward to the edge of the clearing and abruptly stopped. Then he took a grudging step forward – Raydo was behind him, holding the crossbow to the back of his head.

ƺ

"*All* things can change," Raydo's voice crackled like a blackening ember, "Even the face of Falco. Certainly he'll *look* different with an arrow sticking out his eye-socket. I don't know if that will cancel his grand episodic series of voyages but I know it will end the myth of impervious Captain Falco."

Donna stumbled, "No!"

"He's *not* impervious," Zayger barked. "He's the biggest perv in the universe! The perviest!"

Raydo kept his eye on Falco. "I don't know you."

Underbrush crackled low and a beads jangled high as Shayra advanced majestically into the glade. "Raydo, *stop*," her voice shook the trees. Her nimble feet sunk solid and heavy into the moss as she paced toward Captain Falco and leaned, her ear brushed against his nose. "Kill him and you'll kill me too."

Raydo's jaw dropped. He gagged on the many objections rising from his belly but managed only a single word: "...*What?*"

"I know this is hard to understand, but he..." Shayra's voice suddenly wilted as a powerful musk crossed her wide nostrils. "Wow, he really *does* smell good, even his breath – how do you *do* that?"

"I'll *never* tell," Falco snapped his heels, stoically. "You'll have to kill me."

"But I'm trying to *help*-- Never mind. Raydo."

Raydo sneered, "I suppose you're gonna tell me too much blood has been shed? Killing him won't fix anything? Make me no better than him?"

Shayra smiled with a warmth that melted his guts. "No, those are all really stupid reasons to not kill somebody."

"It's true," Claudio added, "they always come back *way* more dangerous after someone says that."

"But he's..." The apprentice drew a deep breath. "It *really pains* me to say this, he's...the-only-one-who-can-save-us." It had pained her to get the words out.

In exasperation, Donna blurted "*That's* what he's been trying to *tell* you *all year!*"

♭

Shayra pulled a flower bulb from her belt and pulled the stem to pop it, puffing a cloud of spores toward Falco's face. "Who *are* you?"

Falco coughed and stuttered. "I... I don't...

know..."

Claudio shook his head grimly. "*I* know who knows. The only one you'll listen to."

He pulled the Falco action figure from his belt and pressed a button. "You may *call* me...*Captain*," it said.

Falco's body imperceptibly shifted into heroic oratory stance. "I am *Captain* Calvin Theseus Falco. *Advocate* of liberty, *bringer* of the noise, *comforter* of unwed mothers, *destroyer* of curfews, *entertainment* of lady-police-officer-bachelorette-parties, *foiler* of--"

Raydo cocked an eyebrow at Donna. "How long does this go on?"

"I think he's going alphabetically."

♭

Everyone froze when they heard the low tolling and saw the small, huddled, mushroom-hooded figure slouch into the clearing. "The time has come for us to reclaim our human heritage. The symbolism of a radiant hero descending from the sky wasn't exactly subtle, but then the tribes of Deia aren't exactly film-critics."

Zayger darted close and squinted, "What's a 'film?' Ayma?"

The apprentice leaned and sniffed. "That's...not Ayma..."

She continued, "But since nuance is an alien concept on this world, the spirits have authorized me to spell it out: F-A-L-C-O."

"Fa-la-la," Raydo said, "We don't spell. *What* are you trying to say?"

Falco advanced toward her. "She's saying

Falco. Falco the registered trademark commodity, 'ask for it by name,' Falco the celebrity. But she's got the wrong guy. Because *I'm Falco* the *Captain*. And *Captain Falco* says--" He held up the action figure, which said: "Inhale my vapor-trail, you slime-weasel."

The mushroom hood of the old priestess rose, her shoulders flared and her arched back straightened, pulling the train of her robe from the ground. "You leave me no choice," she said in a fuller voice, looming like a cobra, long fingers hooked into the seam of her garment "Now I show *everyone*--"

Raydo, Zayger and Claudio ducked and covered their eyes. "No!"

She tore the tendriled cloak of rags away and shed it lifeless to the ground, emerging to her full height and strength, Athena in her sharp and shining assassin gear. She swiveled her angular jaw, reflecting the onlookers one by one in her cold metallic shades.

Zayger blushed and giggled. "What a relief."

Raydo nodded. "Yeah, *that* was scary."

Athena fixed her gaze on Bayla. "Well?"

A wind whistled through the reeds.

Then suddenly Bayla burst into laughter, the rough and husky bell-ringing laugh that recast the forest leaves in jeering carnival colors. Soon they were all laughing, while the icy assassin cast her piercing stare around to no avail.

"Wow," Donna peered, "does *gravity* know your breasts are defying it like this?"

Claudio giggled, "Did you pry that costume off Madonna's microwavable corpse?"

"*Captain*," she snapped.

Falco grinned thoughtfully. "Yeah, MTV called, they want their 1983 back."

Claudio swished and shook his hand. "Swish – *boom*," they said.

Zayger sputtered, "You're-sexy-and-terrifying-like-a-vulva-with-a-hundred-fangs-and-a-hunter-shrinks-plunging-through-endless-darkness-and-his-spine-melts-but-he-grows-an-exoskeleton-of-spikes-and-scales. Swish – *boom!*"

Athena raised an eyebrow, perplexed, "*That* was-- This is a *girl*, right? Doesn't she need, you know...electro-shock therapy?"

Bayla was still laughing, the quake of her abdomen rustling musical beads, but Claudio realized there was something else, another sound, unfamiliar, in the woods. It was quiet, *trun*-sha, *trun*-sha, *trun*-sha, but growing louder and he couldn't determine a direction. The noise was part mechanical triumph and part forest pain.

And then it was there, surrounding them, the sound marched into sight – a ring of insectoid robots, acid-gray against the purples of the forest. They stood six foot, curved locust bodies on spiney legs with scythe-arms and tiny heads. A single glowing eye, danger-orange, peered from each gray plastic face.

Gasps and a hush fell over the Deians.

"With these two hands I could kill everyone here," Athena said, raising her flattened hands like dueling-knives. "The hunters, the village, the animals, even the trees. I can kill Deia. And you know it. But in the hope of a peaceful transition, I've brought helpers. So." She turned to the priestess again. "The fate of this small and fragile world is in your big, ugly hands. Priestess of Deia. Choose your next words *delicately*."

Bayla walked up, swaying and smiling broadly. "I'll tell you a secret..." she beckoned Athena closer. Then she drew back and threw her full weight into a single fist to the assassin's jaw. Athena's spike heels dug into the moss as her body arched back and slammed to the ground.

ß

The assassin sat up, shook her head and stood, readjusting her sunglasses. "Attempt at diplomacy. Check," her lips pulled to a sharp, tight grin, she rotated her head to pop a kink in her long neck. "And what a relief."

Falco sneered. "You think ten of these plastic grasshoppers can take on the whole village?"

"No. Ten of these machines will keep *you* *here*. Long enough for the other ninety to take *out* the whole village."

Claudio's eyes widened, his desperate glance cast toward the circle of hump-tents. *Trun*-sha, *trun*-sha, *trun*-sha, a rhythmic crunch of underbrush, and through the trees he could see three ranks of synchronized mechanical soldiers surrounding the campsite. He launched himself toward it, but a cold curved plastic forearm hooked his neck, then pinned him to the ground.

"Stay," the assassin hissed sharply. "And you, priestess of Deia. No laughter now? No secret?"

"I have nothing to say to you," Bayla said

coolly.

"Well I have a secret for you. I'll be relocating these hippies to the refugee planet? But the luckiest ones will be those who die fighting *today*. Jackbots. Attack," she said, and the village erupted in sound.

Low war-whoops from hunters, defiant high-pitched keening from gardeners, and above it the frightened cries of children. Bayla's green eyes remained calm as the violence began. She could see the distant flashing of teeth and blades against the cold gray plastic of mechanical soldiers.

Clamped to the ground, Claudio struggled to turn himself face down, then dug his fingers into the blue moss and pushed with all his might. "Captain..." he grunted, *"Please. Go be Falco."*

Falco grinned. "It sounds like an order. But I can't refuse." Three graceful leaps and his foot touched down between Claudio's shoulders, with a mighty press he launched the Captain over the machines' swiping arms. Their momentary distraction was Donna's chance to dart through between them, and the two vaulted into the village fray.

The robot shoved Claudio's face back into the dirt, then spazzed and lost its grip. A metal arrow from Raydo's crossbow had pierced its orange eye through to the back of its head. In a black flash of shining feathers the young hunter sprinted and bounded over its crumpling chassis toward the village. Zayger whooped and followed.

Claudio stood and squared his broad shoulders. "You and me," he said.

Athena laughed. "I've heard about you. The ensign who failed to die for his captain. And now you're a stag king who wants to die for this village. You won't have that satisfaction. I've told my jackbots not to kill you. We take you alive. To the refugee planet, for the rest of your days. So say goodbye to your priestess. *This* space fantasy is *over*."

"No..." Claudio's eyes again scanned the village. He could see Raydo in black rallying the adults while lashing out with his metal crossbow. Donna's figure flashed in spin-kicks, popping robot shrapnel into the air. And off to one side, a dense thicket of thorny gray mechanical limbs, thrusting and churning, from its center something glinted.

Falco's teeth.

The heroic grin.

The Captain was dancing again.

Windmills and baby-spins, jackhammers – break-dancing. Elevating on a pile of broken robot parts, his head and shoulders emerged from the fray. Then he pulled his arms in tight to his sides and began bobbing and kicking. River-dance.

"He's quite something, isn't he?" Athena smiled. "Go ahead and watch, fan-boy, if that's what you do with your last moments of freedom. But even *he* can't protect the whole village."

"Kayno," he heard Bayla's voice. Looking over he realized, no, it was the apprentice. "Here. With us."

Claudio wrenched his eyes from Falco and saw the priestesses digging their heels into the moss, shaking their arms loosely. He walked to Bayla's side and hung his head.

"Oh!" the assassin laughed. "Now *you're* gonna dance too!"

"Rhythm," Shayra said. *"Listen* for it."

Claudio closed his eyes and filtered out the battle-sounds of the village. He filtered out the babbling stream and the chattering forest. Somewhere inside he heard it, his own heart. Then it was in his palms, clapping rhythmically against the leather straps crossing his chest. The beat was joined with percussion, the priestesses jangling their beads. And then crowning this, a whistle from Shayra, long notes broken by bursts of short chirps, a pattern, a code.

And a rumbling from below.

The ground grumbled, as if awakening.

Then it quaked, and roared.

Opening his eyes he saw a flash of the assassin's face, white with fear.

The animals came.

Skittering jackanapes slashed through the village and glade like the foam of a wave, followed by a stream of jowns and cloakers.

"Deians to the trees!" Shayra shouted as the forest unleashed a flood of stampeding snuffaloes. Claudio looked, the villagers were scrambling up branches while the storm of blue bison smashed through the mechanical army. Only one person remained on the ground and it was Falco, still dancing.

Then the forest floor quaked harder, heaving with thunderous thuds. A herd of shaggy smellophants burst through the village and glade, trampling the broken robots to powder.

And they were gone, the rumbles receded to mild tremors, and stillness.

Silence.

ß

Claudio blinked around. Where there had been machines, now were only pathetic gray piles of plastic splinters and dust. Falco and Donna were striding from the village, her clothing once again shredded to ribbons and his uniform immaculate, neither had been hurt. Behind them he could see the Deians climbing down from the trees, Raydo and Zayger reuniting stray children with their parents.

The assassin trembled with rage. *"You..."* she hissed at the priestess.

"Here we are," Bayla smiled, gesturing the others to stillness.

Athena charged. Bayla squared her feet and lowered her brow like a hockey goalie as the assassin attacked, long limbs darting and slashing. With her thick arms and massive hands the priestess blocked and brushed the onslaught of jabs and strokes, pounding with her fists but unable to make contact. Athena wove and managed to kick a spiked heel into Bayla's thigh, the priestess grunted and fell to one knee.

The sight of her blood gripped Falco and he jolted forward, but he folded in two as Donna hooked an arm around his waist. "Captain, no!"

"Damnit unhand me!" he shouted.

Shiny sharp white knuckles hit the priestess and her hard landing rocked the forest floor. Athena drew a pistol and pointed it at Bayla's head. "You'll still be a stunning exhibit. But now I'm thinking, definitely stuffed."

With a stunning pirouette, Falco twisted free

of Donna. She helplessly snatched at his shirt as he danced himself into Athena's space, knocking the pistol away. "Maybe you should focus on the *main* attraction."

He winked.

She attacked, hands chopping, feet stabbing, and he spun and dodged in his bullfight ballet. With a spin he slammed the back of his heel into her side, popped a couple punches into her abdomen, then switched to a left-hand lead and Latin flair to dodge her responsive onslaught, now growing sloppy with rage.

Seeing Donna lurch forward he shouted "Lieutenant *stand down, that's an order.*" A hand skimmed his hair and he froze for a second, lips twisted in annoyance. Then a fist stamped his forehead, a kick deflated his stomach, the forest seemed to flip and he was on his back, straddled, her sharp knees crushing into his ribs and knuckles pounding him into the moss. She pulled the action figure from his belt and lashed him with it. Then she held it to Falco's ear, it said: "Kids, remember – *real* heroes drink the milk of a cow."

Tossing the figure aside with a smirk, Athena drew a knife. "Like I said, I don't *need* help to kill you all. The jackbots would have done it cleaner. But truth be told I like this better. Now. I wonder if it's really true that Falco can't be scarred. *This* famous eyebrow--"

"NOOOOOO!" Donna shouted, vaulting at Athena, catching the assassin off guard with a kick to the head that sent her reeling. Then the lieutenant leapt, landing both heels down hard on Athena's wrists, twisting, a sickening sound – the crackle of bone shattering in spirals. Jumping, she stomped twice, caving Athena's knees backward. Then she clamped the assassin's neck-line and belt, lifted and crunched her lower spine over a knee. Casting the broken body aside, she darted to Falco. "Captain...are you alright?"

Athena's fingers clawed and grasped her pistol, with a wince she lifted it. "Eat protein—I mean *proton*, Falco!" Claudio kicked the pistol away but too late, she'd already fired.

Twisting, Donna blocked the bullet between her shoulders, and slumped down into the Captain's lap.

ß

Falco cradled her in his arms. "Lieutenant!"

"Captain!" she said breathlessly "Can I call you...?"

"Yes, whatever you want, just hold on..."

"Jack...rabbit...hammer..."

"Um...right, yes, let's keep it down but you can call me that now..."

"My first day aboard the Exogamy...we passed in the hall, you were striding so *urgently* and there was...a little piece of spinach on one of your teeth, and...I wanted to *be* that spinach. Close to you always..."

"I was urgently seeking dental floss to eliminate that...leafy cling-on."

"And then at the Easter Social, when you asked if those were space-pants I was wearing...and we went to your quarters...and oh my stars...then we played dress-up in your ice-cream sundae topping bar..."

Falco's eyes darted around, the others were visibly disturbed. "Ahem. Yes."

"We'll...play again?"

"Yes, we'll play again. With extra sprinkles, just hold on..." Falco raised his jaw to the wide sky. "If you can hear me...Santa Claus..?" Donna beamed brightly. Then the twinkle dulled from her eyes and her head dropped back, lifeless.

"NOOOOOOOOOOOOOOO!" The Captain's cry summoned a swirl of blue smutterflies in a vortex that levitated pink leaves from the ground and the glade was a twisting hurricane of sad sunset purple. Crocketts chirped like violins and reedy grasses horned mournful strains. Distant snuffaloes lowed and jackanapes yowled like bagpipes. Abdomens throughout the village clenched and eyelids quivered. Then for a second all suspended in silence as Falco drew breath to continue, "OOOOOO-odelay-odeloo-odelay-odelOOOOOOOOOOOOOO!"

And with Falco's space-famous yodel everyone felt the clamping of their gut rustle upward, tightening their chests and throats, erupting into irrepressible sobs and tears. Truly his Hidden Valley yodeling championship medal was well deserved. The Captain's mighty voice finally hollowed out, the spiraling smutterflies dispersed like souls into the sky and pink leaves drizzled dejected to the ground. "No..." he breathed, and it was all the onlookers could do to restrain themselves from bursting into applause.

The forest slumped silent, spent, exhausted.

Claudio desperately wiped his face, the scene had been so blurry and beautiful, but as a lifelong fan he had to get one clear glimpse of it. As the image took shape, he noticed something and advanced. "Captain... This isn't blood. It's motor-oil."

Falco sniffed his hand. Donna blinked her eyes. They stood up and brushed themselves off. "Well I *told* you she was a fembot." He wiped the oil on her sleeve. "And I told *you* you were a fembot. *Why* does anybody *argue* with me? *Ever?*"

"Captain, I didn't know," she said breathlessly.

"Silly robot."

"Errors like this deserve swift discipline."

"Spanking won't fix the past..." Falco muttered grimly, "B*elieve* me."

"The pod-crash must have...scrambled my circuits..."

"Well," he smirked, "now that we're finally agreed you're a fembot, we can scramble your circuits any way we like."

"Oh Captain, you *do* have a way with machines..."

The young huntress wiped a tear and put an arm around Claudio. "It's just like one of his stories..."

"Yes," Claudio sighed, tired. "It's just like *all* his stories."

Approaching from the village, Raydo surveyed the scene. "What do we do about *her?*"

"I'm glad you brought that up," Athena said, smiling from the ground. "Now that you've learned so many valuable lessons about yourselves, you'll spare my life so *I* can learn the true value of mercy. I mean...surely you don't think I would heal up and start killing you off one by one in some later adventure..?" She laughed, then winced in pain. "Inconceivable, right?"

"She's got a point." Falco said.

Donna walked over and pressed a finger into Athena's trachea until it crackled. "No. That would be pre*post*erously stupid. Keefer. Bury her body over there. And her head over there. There's no sequel for *this* one."

"Yes," the huntress said, "But... Raydo..?"

"Fine, I'll help. But only if I can call you Zayger."

"Yes! *Zayger.* ...Captain?"

Falco smiled. "Kid, you've earned it. Put 'er there." He offered his arm and the huntress enthusiastically punched it. Then Raydo and Zayger dragged the body toward the stream. Shayra nodded at Bayla, and walked off toward the village.

ƺ

"Well?" Falco flicked a bit of dirt off his cheek. His face and uniform were remarkably unsullied. A breeze rustled his skirt and brushed a branch aside to let a ray of sunlight wrap the Captain's head in a glowing halo. He gracefully shifted into a heroic pose. "It's been a space-blast, but I'm ready for the continuing adventures of Captain Falco."

Claudio shaded his eyes. "...But Federation Loan owns your contract. And they foreclosed on the planet Earth."

"Oh, right. Hm." Falco thoughtfully ran a finger along his jaw-line, as if the jut of it might remind him of something. He nodded. "Then there's only one thing I can do. If I want to be Captain I'll have to...destroy Federation Loan and *save* the planet Earth. Why not? I've saved every *other* world – why not mine?"

Donna stared wide and blinking. "He...*said* it. He said he would do it..."

"Wow," Claudio smiled. "You're right. He *really will* save the Earth."

Falco winked. "Of course. With my looks? My moves? A pneumatic fembot and a handsome security officer?"

Claudio shook his head. "I can't."

"Wait, you haven't heard what I have to say... Something I've never said before."

"...Well?"

"Claudio."

"You...you *learned* my *name?* ...Wow..."

"Claudio Rivera. You, young man, have a destiny ahead of you. To boldly die in humiliating, bladder-draining terror for a noble cause."

Donna piped in helpfully, "Captain, we don't say 'bladder-draining' anymore, the correct term is...'honorable discharge.'"

"I stand corrected."

"I..." Claudio stared off into the purple forest a moment. "You've always been my hero. I'd forgotten, but seeing you save this world today...even if you were saving it *from* 'Falco'... Anyway, you're my hero and now I remember why. But I've promised to be *their* hero, and there's one last thing I have to do. It's time for the Bollox hunt."

ß

Falco glanced around, and confided, "I've lived a year in the forest and never seen another of those blue monsters. What makes you think one will show up tonight?"

Shayra paced slowly into the clearing with a large, shaggy blue fur. "Are you ready?"

Claudio nodded. "Yes."

Falco lifted an eyebrow as she wrapped it around Claudio's feet, then pulled the suit up over his body. "Whoa, wait, the Bollox is Kayno?"

Donna stepped up defensively, "You're gonna kill him?"

Shayra's rhythmic words rippled through the trees. "Kayno never dies. Tonight, Kayno sheds his old skin and reveals his new face. The Bollox, ancient criminal of the forest, will pay the price..."

"Claudio don't pay for this," Donna snapped.

"Of all the pointless ways for a security officer to die," Falco shook his head, "And I've seen some really, *really*-- Look. There's a maneuver, the old dine-and-dash, we--"

"No Captain. On the day we arrived I told her *you* should be Kayno. But when Bayla whispered to me, Kayno's destiny... I knew that was *my* destiny."

Bayla stepped forward from the treeline. "He

volunteered for a gruesome death to save others, to save *you*, Calvin. Isn't that what you wanted from him?"

Donna squinted, curious "But don't you...have any *feelings* about this?"

"He knows I do." She drew close to Claudio and breathed his scent deeply. "The spirits, the stars, the Interstellar Syndicate and Calvin Theseus Falco brought you to me. My last Kayno, and the one who taught me the most. Thank you."

"But you're gonna *kill him!*" Falco interjected. "For the first time in my life I feel like maybe... Like I don't understand women..."

Donna gasped. "That's *not* true."

"You're a robot," Claudio reminded her.

"Oh. Right. But still, there's a ninety-nine point eight percent chance that he *definitely* understands women."

"Never tell me the odds. And *this...bizarre* situation is...is not about *me*." Falco's face twisted, perplexed, hearing those words in his own voice was more surreal than anything he'd encountered on this planet. *"Wow..."*

"There is one thing I need from you." Claudio looked at Falco.

"Of course, I'll leave your misguided fashion blunders out of my report."

"Don't write what's happened here, any of it. Don't let them know about the planet of Deia."

Falco paused. Then nodded. "I swear it by the abundant man-breasts of Santa."

They locked their pinky-fingers and solemnly tugged.

♮

Returning with Raydo, Zayger bashfully nodded to Claudio. "Kayno."

"Zayger." Claudio offered his arm. Zayger punched it.

"It's been an honor," Raydo nodded.

"If you hunt the Bollox with that, you will *not* succeed."

Raydo stood sullenly a moment. Then he tossed his crossbow into the brush, unclasped his black feathered cloak and cast it off. Except for the leather eyepatch, and a few creases and scars, he looked very much like that boy Claudio had met a year before. "Here we are."

Claudio laid a hand on Raydo's shoulder. "Here we are. Kayno." They embraced.

He cast a last glance toward the village, which was being quickly disassembled. The hump-tents were peeled from their skeleton frames, the tools bundled and tied, the hunters and gardeners worked with a quiet, dignified efficiency. Now each face had a name and a story, some triumph, some loss, and he smiled recalling some of the ways he'd helped.

Then Claudio swept his arms out wide and addressed the surrounding trees. "Mother land, father sky, spirits of the forest and the dead. For the community's toll on the woodland this last thirteen moons, let the responsibility be mine. I am the killer and I am the Bollox. The fugitive will face justice. Let the innocent be spared and delivered to a new home."

Shayra nodded. "Raise him."

♭

Raydo and Zayger lifted Claudio horizontally and the priestesses bound his hands into tight fists with leather strings, then tied hooves over them. Bayla kissed him one last time, then tied a leather strap between his teeth.

Claudio was lowered to the ground, lightly closed his eyes and took a deep breath while Bayla hefted a large stone. Then with all her might she heaved it to the earth, crackling the bones of his right foot. He winced, but quickly regained control of his breathing. Then he was raised again and large hooves were fastened over his feet. Finally the bearded bollox mask was fastened over his head, the seven-pointed antlers protruding.

"The Bollox will stand," Shayra said.

They stood him up and he stumbled, the hunters caught him.

"Zayger, gather the hunters. Tell them the Bollox-hunt begins when they hear the whistle." Then Shayra looked at Claudio. "It's time."

The shaggy blue monster nodded, then hobbled, Ra*shrump, ra*shrump, ra*shrump,* three times in a circle, getting his bearings and picking up speed. Ra*shrump*-ra*shrump*-ra*shrump.* Finally the antlered beast lumbered off into the forest, with the others staring after him.

♭

"There goes our boy," Falco wrapped an arm around Donna's waist, "all grown up and dressed like Cookie-Monster, limping off to his horrible death. It reminds me of my first mission... I had just--"

"NO," Shayra snapped, "We *don't* need your story right now."

Bayla laid a hand on her shoulder. "*He* needs to hear his story."

Shayra scowled at Falco, but finally said "Fine."

"I had just graduated from the Academy, received my assignment, security officer on the shuttle Proboscis, and a mission came in – land of the luscious lava-lampreys, certain doom. And as we launched I looked back, my beloved academy sweetheart Magellen, she'd climbed up a flagpole. Tears in her eyes. I couldn't stand to see her like that. So I fought my way onto the bridge, knocked out the captain and the crew, grabbed the controls, turned on the smoke-jets and spelled in giant letters across the sky... 'Magellen I'm dumping you... Keep my Duran Duran records...away from direct sunlight or excessive heat in case I survive. Sincerely... Interstellar Syndicate ensign thirty-four seventeen dot three Falco comma Calvin Theseus...'"

"I've never read that story," Donna brushed her nose against his ear.

"I've never told it before." He turned to Bayla. "But seeing that look in your eyes...the look I got from Magellen on the flagpole...you love him..."

"Yes, the priestess loves Kayno, so it's always been. But I am not priestess anymore. And he is not Kayno anymore." Bayla's voice was thin and whispery.

"So you kill him."

"Calvin. You see death as an ugly fiancée, following you around, waiting for you to slip up and she'll drag you across the altar."

"No, I... Alright, yes. I do."

"Death to you is the end of what you love most. The adventures of Falco. But what we love most is the *life of the community*. And the natural community does not live in plot-lines and victorious climaxes. It lives in circles, cycles – we borrow from the community and we return to the community."

"That's an awfully friendly way of saying you're gonna kill a sweet, wholesome man and eat him."

"The skin of Kayno is a suit the spirits wear, to protect us. The spirits must leave one body and choose another so that Kayno can live on with the strength to support the tribe."

"I'm not talking about *Kayno*, his name is *Claudio Rivera*."

Bayla picked up Ayma's heavy robes and wrapped them around her shoulders, her wide and massive frame becoming visibly smaller. "Kayno never dies," she murmured, pulling the mushroom hood over her head.

Falco demanded, "*His name is--*"

Donna clamped him, "STOP IT, Captain. *She knows* – can't you see it? I'm a machine and I can see she's hurt."

Reaching into a pocket of the cloak, Bayla pulled out the pipe, so small in her large hands, and stared at it. "His name was Claudio Rivera..."

Shayra blew a whistle. "The Bollox hunt begins."

"Bayla..." Falco said, "I'm sorry." But he

already knew she wasn't Bayla anymore.

ß

"*I* am Bayla now," the former apprentice grimly intoned, "And you will honor your promise to leave and tell no one of our life here."

"He's incapable of lying." Donna nodded.

"But I am not incapable of *sharing*...my feelings in song. One sad yodel for a fallen--"

"NO," her voice shook the forest. "Yodel on the ship, yodel all the way home - this forest has been polluted enough."

"You're the captain here." He nodded respectfully. "I understand."

"You have never understood this place. You will jut your famous jaw into the next episode and the next and the next. And your syndicated series of voyages will continue like this never happened."

"That's not true," Donna objected, "He's never learned the name of a security officer before."

"They always die before I can get to know them."

"Can you *really* see his future? He'll have more missions?"

The priestess heaved a weary sigh, then shook her dark curls, raised her small chin and closed her eyes. "Yes, he'll dismantle Federation Loan, restore the Syndicate, launch another five year mission, discover the Zero-G Spot, accidentally time-travel, search for--"

"Stop," Falco raised a hand. "All I want to know is that the adventure continues." Falco bent to pick up the action figure. "And I want you to have this... If ever you people yearn to grow up and get real. It will guide you." The old priestess slowly shuffled over, received the figure and slipped it inside a fold of her cloak.

"Well?" Donna laid a hand on Falco's chest. "Ship to get home? Check. Security officer dead? Check. Not one hair out of place? Check."

"Space-babe on my arm? Check."

She rubbed a nubile hip against his muscular thigh. "Is that how you like it, Captain?"

He grinned boyishly, a ray of sunshine glinted off one of his perfect teeth. "Check. World to save? Check."

"I'd say we're ready to boldly go. What do *you* say, Captain?"

Falco took a deep breath. The heroic jaw and defiant sideburns, the dancer's frame sweeping to a new valiant grandeur. "*Engage.*" He and Donna charged off into the forest, toward Athena's ship.

ꝅ

The priestess pulled up a pipe and dug into a pouch for a pinch of tree-bark to fill it. Humming a low note she waited, a buzzing alerted her to the approach of an insect and she hummed till it was within reach. Then she snapped out her arm and caught it between thick fingers. Cracking it in two produced a spark and she inhaled deeply from the pipe. "At last..."

"Ayma."

"Bayla," she exhaled a cloud of smoke. "You've chosen an apprentice?"

"Yes, I'll tell her tonight."

"We'll be three and one."

The priestess bent low to take a final sniff of the ground and gather some handfuls of dust, which she gently poured into a leather pouch and tied to her belt. Rising, she glanced back to where the village had been, it was gone without a trace. "We could have been torn apart in this last thirteen moons. All the pain and privation...you let it happen. Why?"

"The space-people came, disruption was inevitable. And so I chose...that exposure to their ways could be a reminder of why we *must* be who we are."

"...I understand it now. We're all back where we're supposed to be. And... I feel it. The Bollox is dead. Raydo is chosen. Kayno for thirteen moons..."

"One thing will change. Becoming Ayma, the priestess is allowed to alter one law. This last thirteen moons, I've made up my mind. It is not only the moon's year that ends tonight, the sun's year ends as well. This alignment has not occurred for eight years and will not occur again for another eight years. Only when that happens will we hunt the Bollox again."

"So Raydo will live."

"Yes."

"Thank you." The priestess embraced her and kissed the top of her mushroom hood. Then she extended a hand and the old woman took it. "...What rule was changed when the last Bayla turned Ayma?"

"She forever abolished those horrible beehive hairstyles."

"Spirits be praised."

"Here we are."

"Here we are."   They left the glade and walked toward their new sanctuary.

Silently the blue moss of the forest floor sponged, swallowing the footprints they'd left behind.   The grasses of the clearing tentatively uncurled again, sifting the gray plastic dust down, and clouds gathered overhead, heavy with the promise of a cleansing rain.

"Peet?" a curlibird's chirp flicked through the silence. "Peet? Peet?"

"*Re*peet."

EXTRA FEATURES

INTERVIEW WITH j. SNODGRASS
BY PHIL S. STEIN

Snodgrass welcomes me at the door of his house in black combat boots, blue jeans and a Nine Inch Nails t-shirt. He leads me past the living room where his stunning wife Elizabeth smiles amid a blurry, babbling bustle of children (four of them, I find out). In some noise and confusion I get brief introductions, then he leads me upstairs.

Snodgrass's tiny office is mostly shelves – a massive library of vinyl records, films and books. So many books. History, mythology, religion, no novels. The remaining wall space is taken up with large framed posters, the screaming face from Pink Floyd's *The Wall* looms horrifically above his desk, beside it a twisted torso labeled "The Sisters of Mercy." Other walls have *Natural Born Killers* and *Young Guns II*. He smirks and says I've stepped inside his brain. But it reminds me more of a monastic cell, the desk an altar. He grins. "Yeah. I lead a secret double life as a monk." Then in mock ritual he opens a window, sets in a box-fan and lights a cigarette.

PSS : So. Where did this idea come from?

TjS : I wanted to write a story again, it had been many, many years of studying and teaching and writing about ancient religions and mythologies. This is an extension of that, in story form, and there was all this stuff I really wanted to fit into it. Daniel Quinn [author of *Ishmael* and *The Invisibility of Success*] is obviously the biggest influence, I'm always looking for new ways to share what I've learned from him.

PSS : Right, the "Leavers" and "Takers"?

TjS : Yeah. Tribal cultures who let the land control itself, and where resources are shared. And "civilized" societies that take control of the land and set up social pyramids. And another of my favorite books is Riane Eisler's *The Chalice and the Blade* which makes a parallel observation, about ancient "partnership" societies of gender balance and cooperation with habitat, and "dominator" societies of male primacy and exploitation of the environment. So I wanted to write a story about a meeting of these two cultures.

PSS : What about the religious elements? Priestesses and such?

TjS : When we moved to Buffalo I had a semester off from teaching, and decided to launch a serious investigation of how these themes of gender and "nature" are deeply embedded in the ritual roots of what we call "mythology." So I finally read Robert Graves' *The White Goddess* and Sir James Frazer's *The Golden Bough* both containing explorations of ancient societies on the brink – leavers/partners with female priestesses ruling and male figureheads replaced at regular intervals. Then kings take control and the societies become taker/dominators. ...And now that I think about it, I should have said I was trying to combine *five* books, since re-reading Joseph Campbell's *The Hero with a Thousand Faces* was definitely an influence. Or *six* books since... Anyway I'll stop there. So much stuff I wanted to say, and the real challenge was to get as much of this in as possible, while hopefully still keeping the focus on interesting characters and relationships.

PSS : I assume *Star Trek* was an influence as well.

TjS : Definitely! I grew up *Star Wars* but I converted. As preparation for this project, I immersed myself in it, watching every episode of the Original Series. *Star Trek* is utopian, a noble ideal of respecting diversity. And the Prime Directive requires that they don't interfere with the development of other cultures. And yet in almost every episode they *do* interfere, so it's also *dystopian*. They're "good people," but they're also the "bad guys," and that fascinates me. So I wanted to create characters like that. In my story the Syndicate is this evil corporation, but Falco, Donna, Claudio, they're not "good" or "bad," they're just childish.

PSS : So after all that research – how did you get started?

TjS : The first step in writing this story was to write a different book, *Romancing the Minotaur: Sex and Sacrifice and some Greek Mythology*, which looks at the fall of the ancient "matriarchal" culture of Crete, and how it was commandeered in the reign of Minos and then parodied in the myth of Theseus. I briefly considered setting this story in an ancient Cretan city, but wanted the forest to play an active role, so set it in a sort of pre-Crete. And this enabled me to draw in some details from the Iroquois, the Druids and Celts, and other cultures. I didn't make up any stuff about this tribe on Deia – part of the fun of writing this was to create an "alien" culture using elements of ancient human societies. And when that book was done, I wrote this as a stage script, a sort of low-budget 1980s space fantasy.

PSS : Why rewrite it as a novel?

TjS : When someone likes my stage-writing, teaching, whatever, I want to give them a book. But I think people are scared off by these massive ancient histories with hundreds of footnotes. They're written to be fun! But that's not what people read for fun, except me. So I felt like it was time for a novel. But what story would I tell, if I could tell any story in the whole, whatever, universe? This one. And four years after writing it, this play is no closer to a stage. So I can share it this way.

PSS : Did you make changes?

TjS : Not really. I thought about it – this is a different medium, compared to stage-writing, so much space! More characters, flashbacks, waterfall-jumps, anything is possible. But I wanted to keep it focused on the characters, the relationships. I don't read novels, and when I did, I only really liked the dialogue, that's when I feel like the story is moving forward. Not during some long exposition or description. I did make one addition, at the last minute, of the robot army. Really because it was an additional chance to establish the relationship with the forest and animals. That's the most significant development, I think, from the script – the novel format gave me a chance to incorporate nature as a major character, not just a scenic backdrop.

PSS : You wrote this four years ago. Do you think it's timely now?

TjS : Yeah, the characters, dialogue, relationships – all of that was written in 2015, before I recall Donald Trump even being a political candidate. And it's popped into my head a few times over these last four years, how some of the material in this story has been, I don't know, distorted by that. There's a playful attitude toward sexism here, which I wrote as a joke about the 1960s. The story never sides with Falco's chauvinism, but it also never punishes him for it. There's a playful attitude toward fascism too, which might not be so timely right now. Do I think it's timely? I set out to write a good story, and if I succeeded, then a good story is timely regardless of today's, whatever, political weather.

PSS : Where do the character names come from?

TjS : Falco comes from Austrian rapper Falco, whose album *Einzelhaft* I was listening to a lot when I started writing this. Because the story's about destiny, there's the obvious reference to John Calvin, the Christian reformer who proposed the doctrine of predestination. Also of course the boy from Bill Watterson's Calvin and Hobbes, and the play does contain a reference to his alter-ego Spaceman Spiff. Theseus is famous for the Minotaur story, but there were also other obscure legends of Theseus as an adventurer and womanizer.

Donna is named for Donna Summer, a pioneer of electric disco. The name Claudio literally means "cripple," and I knew I wanted the character's foot to get broken in the end. Robert Graves wrote a good deal about the limping king. I don't understand what it means, but someday it'll dawn on me and I'll be glad to have included it.

Bayla went through several names, and the name was only finalized once I'd established naming rules for all the Deian characters. Ayma comes from the Arabic word *Umma,* meaning "mother" and "tribe." Shayra is from *Sarai,* an old Babylonian word for "princess." Not in the sense of a king's daughter but actually meaning apprentice moon priestess. Once these were established, it became obvious that the name in between should begin with a "B." As I wrote the first entrance of the two young hunters, I pulled two names from sixties music – one from Zager and Evans, "In the Year 2525," and the other from James Rado, one of the lyricists of the musical *Hair.* Athena is named after the coldest and most impersonal of the Greek goddesses, born not of a mother's womb but out of Zeus' head.

PSS : So, a lot of musical references. Were there certain songs that you listened to while writing?

TjS : Stevie Nicks, I'd just got the *Crystal Visions* compilation and the song "Planets of the Universe" was my hype song when preparing to write. Duran Duran's *Paper Gods* came out while I was working on this and I played it to death. And I also collect vinyl records of German pop from the 1980s – Alphaville, Falco, Nena, I was listening to that a lot. I made a sort of soundtrack playlist:

Stevie Nicks – Planets of the Universe
Falco – Vienna Calling
Donna Summer – I Feel Love
Duran Duran – Change the Skyline
Alphaville – Sexyland
Stevie Nicks – Rooms on Fire
Falco – Falco Rides Again
Kate Bush – Rocket's Tail
Alphaville – Fallen Angel
Scooter – Jigga Jigga!
Duran Duran – The Universe Alone
Hair Original Broadway Cast – The Flesh Failures

PSS : The book ends where it begins.

TjS : This is a story about destiny. There's a clockwork mechanism to it - every character is on a certain path at the start, going in a certain direction. The arrival of the Syndicate officers and then the Collector threaten to break the machine, but it fixes itself. In the end everyone is where they were meant to be. The big twist is that nothing has changed.

PSS : Anything else?

TjS : Yeah. When you're writing a script, if it goes into production you know the director's gonna study it, performers are gonna have to memorize it, it's gotta stand up to close study. And then the lighting operator is gonna have to see it eight, ten, fifteen times, whatever. And I think about that when I write, the light person making six bucks an hour to watch the same show over and over and over again. So I challenge myself – can I make the light operator laugh on their tenth time watching? Some little, I don't know, riddle joke they didn't notice all the times before?

PSS : "Easter Eggs"?

TjS : Yeah, I mean aside from the Easter candy *already* in this book. I'm not thinking of something specific right now, but yeah. I hope this will be a good story someone can enjoy once, have a whatever, one-night-stand with, but my favorite books and films I've had a long and developing relationship with, they get better with revisiting, and I hope this story can be that for someone else.

PSS : Do you think you'll write more of this?

TjS : Maybe. I've got some ideas. But there are so many exciting frontiers to explore – stage, fiction, nonfiction, I'm super-excited to start my next commentary book. But we'll see what happens. We'll see.

EXCERPT FROM

Romancing
THE MINOTAUR:
SEX AND SACRIFICE
AND SOME GREEK MYTHOLOGY

Available wherever.

THE MINOTAUR

One of the earliest visual representations of the Minotaur is an engraving on a tiny gold ornament crafted about two thousand seven hundred years ago. The image centers on a muscular hero in a jockstrap, gripping the horn of a bull-headed man while plunging a blade into his armpit. The Minotaur on the right stands a little shorter than the hero with the head of a bull or stag. Naked except for a belt and bracelet, his right hand hooks the hero's wrist and his left hand grips the blade (while the engraving is small and hard to read, it really looks like the Minotaur is guiding the blade into himself, not pushing it away). There is no aggression or fear in the scene: the hero is not low in a driving lunge, the Minotaur is not bent in defense or defeat.

Behind the hero stands a muscular topless woman wearing an elaborately patterned skirt and headband. One hand hovers open just behind the hero's head while the other is poised to pinch his heroic backside or adjust his jockstrap – it's not exactly clear what her hand is doing down there. But her outstretched arms convey guidance and protection, the hero is under her control. If we stared long enough into this scene, the central figure would fade into the background: the interaction is between the topless woman and the bull-headed man, and the hero is a puppet, pushed by the woman, pulled by the Minotaur.

This ornament was manufactured far from the scene of the Minotaur showdown, about seven hundred years after Theseus lived. Later representations will show significant variations: the monster will become larger and its head more clearly bullish, its bodily stature crouching, dodging or counter-attacking, sometimes holding a boulder (in some depictions, Theseus fights a bull that is not half-man at all, giving rise to a separate legend of his battle with the Bull at Marathon). Some depictions will show only the two combatants while others will surround them with the Cretan princess Ariadne, the goddess Athena and a bunch of teenagers.

A thousand years after the event, an Athenian commemorative coin will feature the Minotaur on one side with a stylized maze on the reverse. The lack of setting in earlier depictions makes it unclear whether the dungeon/maze was always part of the story – no trace of such a structure has ever been found in the ruins of ancient Crete, where the story takes place.

A BULL STORY
-OR-
ANIMAL HUSBANDRY

There are no photographs or videos of the Minotaur fight, no eyewitness reports in newspapers (and if Theseus himself had written a blog-post about his Cretan island safari, how reliable would we consider his report?). The earliest comprehensive Minotaur narratives were written centuries after the fall of classical Greece by Romans who compiled sensational fragments of tall-tales for cheap low-brow entertainment. The writings are a bit cartoonish, with a boyish fixation on lewd and supernatural elements – we could consider these the "locker-room" versions of the story. The following basic Minotaur narrative has been assembled with pieces from Ovid, Plutarch and Pseudo-Apollodorus, all produced in or around the first century of the common era (about fifteen hundred years after the event).

The story begins like many other ancient myths: a wise and mighty Olympian deity is overpowered with lust while spying on some comely teenager, in this case a broad-faced Syrian princess named Europa. The name of the deity in Ovid's account is Zeus, but his description of the earth-shaking god with the three-pronged spear will sound more like the ocean deity Poseidon, who will be central in the rest of the story, so it's possible that Zeus was a later replacement. *"The Father of all Gods whose right hand held a three-pronged thunderbolt, whose slightest nod was an earthquake up to heaven, dropped his royal sceptre and became a bull [with] huge, silky muscles at his neck and silvered dewlaps hanging, small horns as white as if a sculptor's hand had cut them out of pearl... She [Europa] went to him with a gift of daisies to his snow-white lips. He was all joy, tasting the future as he kissed her hands, nor could he straightly control his love: he danced the grasses and rolled his whiteness into golden sands [until the princess] climbed to his back; slowly the god stepped out into the shallows of the beach and with false-footed softness took to sea, swimming against full tide, the girl his captured prize; she, fearful, turned to shoreward, set one hand on his broad back, the other held one horn, her dress behind her fluttered in the wind."* (Ovid, *Metamorphoses*) The white bull landed with Europa on the island of Crete, where he did what Greek gods and heroes do. One of the triplets conceived was called Minos.

"Minos wanted to be king of Crete, but there was opposition. He claimed that he had received the kingship from the gods, and to prove it he said that whatever he prayed for would happen. He made a sacrifice to Poseidon and prayed for a bull to appear from the depths, promising to sacrifice the one that appeared. Poseidon sent a magnificent bull up for him, and he received the kingdom, but he sent the bull to his herds and sacrificed another... Poseidon grew angry at Minos because he did not sacrifice the bull. So he made it savage and made [Minos' wife] Pasiphae lust after the bull." (Apollodorus, *Library*)

Determined to consummate this bestial union, the Cretan queen approached an inventor named Daedalus. *"He constructed a wooden cow, put it on wheels, and hollowed it out. Stripping the skin from a cow, he sewed it around the wooden one. He placed it in the meadow where the bull usually grazed and put Pasiphae inside. The bull came and mated with it."* (Apollodorus, *Library*) And so the Minotaur was born. Minos then forced the inventor to imprison this hulking, sulking creature: *"Blind walls of intricate complexity...led the eye astray by a mazy multitude of winding ways... Daedalus in countless corridors built bafflement, and hardly could himself make his way out, so puzzling was the maze." (*Ovid, *Metamorphoses)*

Poseidon's bull continued to terrorize the Cretans until Heracles dragged it off the island to Marathon, near Athens, and there it terrorized the Athenians (apparently it also learned how to breathe fire). Years later, Minos' son visited Athens and the king was so impressed with this Cretan prince's athleticism that he challenged him to hunt the bull. The prince was slain and Minos, enraged, ordered that every nine years (or some sources say every year), the Athenians *"send seven young men and the same number of young women, all unarmed, as food for the Minotaur, who had been shut up in a labyrinth, which was impossible for someone who entered to get out of, for it closed off its secret exit with complex twists and turns."* (Apollodorus, *Library*)

Enter Theseus, the Athenian king's illegitimate son from a drunken one-night stand (some say Poseidon's son as well), who delighted the Athenians by killing Poseidon's raging bull, then offered to rid them of the Minotaur. He set sail with the next batch of Athenian youth. *"When he arrived in Crete, Minos' daughter Ariadne fell in love with him and offered to help him if he promised to take her back to Athens and make her his wife. After Theseus promised and swore oaths on it, she asked Daedalus to reveal the way out of the labyrinth. At his suggestion she gave a thread to Theseus as he entered. Theseus tied this to the door and went in dragging it behind. He found the Minotaur in the innermost part of the labyrinth and beat him to death with his fists. He got out by following the thread back."* (Apollodorus, *Library*) The old Saxon word for a ball of yarn is "Clew," from which we get the modern word "Clue."

Theseus sabotaged the mighty Cretan fleet, then set sail with princess Ariadne and the Athenian teenagers. They landed on a small island, but what happened next is an ancient mystery. Mythographers generally agree he raped and abandoned the princess. Some say she then hanged herself, others say she was discovered unconscious by the wine-god Dionysus, who took her to be his immortal bride (his wedding gift was a crown of stars, the constellation *Corona Borealis*). Homer says Ariadne had *already* been married to Dionysus, and that upon learning of her affair with Theseus he sent an assassin to kill her. Plutarch, in his biography of Theseus, proposes that there may have been two Ariadnes, one raped or married by Theseus, the other married to Dionysus or a priest of Dionysus. *"There are many different accounts of these events, and of the story of Ariadne, none of which agree in their details."* (Plutarch, *The Rise and Fall of Athens*) Whatever happened, Theseus did not keep his promise to the princess, although there are multiple attestations that Theseus did later marry Ariadne's sister Phaedra, who also apparently hanged herself. (Hyginus, *Fabulae*)

Nobody says that Theseus was the greatest of Greek heroes. Even in Classical Greece he was generally considered a half-assed Heracles (having *literally* lost half his ass on a botched kidnapping mission in Hades, he then had to be rescued by the *real* Heracles). The guy who chopped off Medusa's head and used it to rescue the princess from the seamonster in *Clash of the Titans*? That was Perseus. The guy who escaped the Cyclops, Circe and Sirens? Odysseus. The Trojan Horse? Achilles. Every Greek legend you've ever heard that wasn't about the Minotaur was someone else, not Theseus.

Even Theseus' arch-nemesis, the Minotaur, has had to abandon his old sparring partner and find work elsewhere to stay current, recently accepting cameo roles in Hollywood productions about Perseus. Dissing Theseus hasn't hurt the Minotaur's career, but losing touch with his native Crete reduces the Minotaur to a mindless movie monster (although he *was* particularly terrifying when Jack Nicholson played him in *the Shining*, chasing his son through that maze). Surprisingly, we've yet to see a reality show in which the Minotaur dances the tango or moves in with Vanilla Ice.

One of my favorite board games is called *Minotaurus*, a game built out of Legos that encourages you to change the rules after playing it. The game involves a Minotaur and a movable maze, but none of the characters is Theseus, and so I usually change a rule to add him in. Recently, we've been playing a great board game called *the aMAZEing Labyrinth* with no hero or monster at all. And a nearby church has an outdoor prayer-labyrinth of bricks pounded into the lawn, which the kids enjoy running around in. It's been decades since I saw the movie *Labyrinth*, but I can't stop watching *The Name of the Rose*, where the labyrinthine library hides a killer chimera. These are just a few examples off the top of my head – there are many modern stories that incorporate elements of the Minotaur and the prison-maze.

So why write a book about Theseus and the Minotaur? Not to spoil the ending, but this book is not really about Theseus and the Minotaur at all. As a student of Daniel Quinn, I study what it means to be human, and how that has changed since the transition from migratory foragers to settled farmers. I'm particularly interested in how social and gender dynamics have been shaped by this transition. And while reading Robert Graves and James Frazer I was struck by three topics: 1. Crete, an advanced ancient civilization ruled primarily by women. 2. Ancient kings who were sacrificed after a year in power. 3. Barbaric invaders who overran ancient matriarchal cultures, and the vestiges of feminine power that remained. At some point in the study I was reminded of the Minotaur story, an ideal frame for linking these three topics. Also, having just moved to Buffalo NY, I see totem bison heads *everywhere*, sometimes with human bodies.

And so this book will be organized in three sections, corresponding with the three central figures in the Minotaur story. The first will explore the Cretan queen-priestess and princess-apprentice, how these two characters are actually a single figure at different stages of life, and how she fits into the cultural context of ancient Crete. The second section of this book will explore the Cretan king Minos and the Minotaur (which literally means "Minos-Bull") and how they represent a merger of Cretan island culture with the barbarian mainland culture. The third section of this book will be about Theseus as a representation of the barbaric warriors who finally destroyed Cretan culture, incorporating elements of it into what would later develop into Classical Greek culture. It is the goal of this book that when we return to the Minotaur story at the end, we'll see it with more depth and clarity, and rather than classify it as "Fact" or "Fairy Tale," we'll see that it contains a certain "truth" about this historical transition.

...And the book continues from there.

Romancing
THE MINOTAUR:
SEX AND SACRIFICE AND SOME GREEK MYTHOLOGY

A BRIEF AND COMICAL GLANCE AT THE ROOTS OF GREEK MYTHOLOGY. PSYCHEDELIC DRUGS, SUPERNATURAL SEXUALITY, AND HUMAN SACRIFICE ENTWINE IN THE LEGEND OF A PRINCESS, A HERO AND A MONSTER ON THE ISLAND OF CRETE.

Available wherever.

ALSO BY j. SNODGRASS

"CHAOS"

COLLECTED SPEECHES 2012-2014
"CHAOS IS A DISTURBING, DISCONCERTING, AND
DELICIOUS DIATRIBE. IT WILL STIR UP THE
LITTLE GRAY CELLS IN YOUR HEAD,
GUARANTEED." -DANIEL QUINN, AUTHOR OF
ISHMAEL.

"CHAOS, CHAOS"

COLLECTED SPEECHES 2014-2018
HUMANITY. WHO ARE WE? WHY ARE WE HERE?
HOW DO WE FIT IN? AND HOW HAVE THE
ANSWERS CHANGED AS WE'VE GONE FROM
NOMADIC FORAGERS TO SETTLED FARMERS TO
MODERN CONSUMERS?

NATIVES DISCOVER AMERICA :
AN ANTHROPOLOGICAL STUDY
OF THE "WHITE MAN"

FOR MORE THAN FIVE HUNDRED YEARS,
NATIVES OF THE AMERICAS HAVE BEEN
STUDYING THE MYSTERIOUS "WHITE MAN."
WHO DOES HE THINK HE IS? WHY DOES HE DO
WHAT HE DOES? HOW CAN HE BE SO
DESTRUCTIVE? AND CAN HE LEARN TO LISTEN
TO OTHERS BEFORE IT'S TOO LATE?

GENESIS AND THE RISE OF CIVILIZATION

"A REMARKABLY READABLE AND
ENLIGHTENING VOLUME." –DANIEL QUINN,
AUTHOR OF ISHMAEL.

SNODGRASS INTEGRATES STUDIES OF WORLD
MYTHOLOGIES, ANCIENT NEAR EASTERN TRIBES
AND EMPIRES, ARCHAEOLOGY AND RABBINIC
LEGEND TO READ GENESIS AS A PARABLE FOR
THE AGRICULTURAL REVOLUTION AND GOD'S
COUNTER-REVOLUTION.

LIBEL:
SEX AND SEXUALITY IN THE BIBLE

WARNING: THIS BOOK DOES NOT CONTAIN THE
ANSWER ABOUT WHAT'S "RIGHT" AND
"WRONG" CONCERNING SEX *OR* THE BIBLE –
ONLY TEXTS TO PONDER AND QUESTIONS TO
CONSIDER.

TURNING THE TABLES:
FARMING THE FEEDING IN THE GOSPELS

WHAT DID JESUS EAT?
HOW WAS FOOD GROWN, PREPARED AND
SERVED? WHO WAS DOING THE WORK, AND
WHO WAS GAINING THE WEALTH? WHAT DID
JESUS THINK ABOUT THE RULES OF TABLE
FELLOWSHIP? AND HOW DID HE TURN THE
TABLES?

Made in the USA
Middletown, DE
31 May 2019